A GRAIN OF RICE

NHUNG N. TRAN-DAVIES

A GRAIN OF RICE

Tradewind Books
VANCOUVER • LONDON

Published in Canada in 2018
Published in the USA and the UK in 2019

Text © 2018 by Nhung N. Tran-Davies
Cover illustration © 2018 by Shaoli Wang
Cover design by Elisa Gutiérrez
Book design by Jacqueline Wang

MIX
Paper from
responsible sources
FSC
www.fsc.org
FSC® C016245

The paper is 100% post-consumer recycled and processed chlorine and acid-free.

Printed in Canada by Friesens

2 4 6 8 10 9 7 5 3 1

Cataloguing-in-Publication Data for this book
is available from The British Library.

Library and Archives Canada Cataloguing in Publication

Tran-Davies, Nhung N., author
    A grain of rice / Nhung N. Tran-Davies.

Issued in print and electronic formats.
ISBN 978-1-926890-33-3 (hardcover).--ISBN 978-1-926890-25-8 (softcover).--
ISBN 978-1-926890-49-4 (EPUB)

    I. Title.

PS8639.R38G73 2018   jC813'.6   C2018-904131-5
                                          C2018-904132-3

The publisher thanks the Government of Canada, the Canada Council
for the Arts and Livres Canada Books for their financial support.
We also thank the Government of the Province of British Columbia
for the financial support we have received through
the Book Publishing Tax Credit program
and the British Columbia Arts Council.

 Canada Council **Conseil des Arts**  BRITISH COLUMBIA
for the Arts **du Canada** ARTS COUNCIL
Supported by the Province of British Columbia

  LIVRES CANADA BOOKS

To Kenya, Monet, and Sage.
May you always live life with
hope, courage, resilience
and kindness.

This book would not have been possible without my publishers Michael Katz and Carol Frank believing in me. I am forever grateful for the opportunity to tell my story.

Many thanks also to my wonderful editor Shed Simas for helping me get to the heart of my story, and also the rest of the Tradewind team—Viktoria Cseh, Jacqueline Wang, Hilary Leung, Colin Campbell, Elisa Gutierrez and Shaoli Wang.

Special thanks also to my friends and family for sharing their recollections of our past—Phuong Nguyen, Son Nguyen, Yan Chen, Thanh Ho, Dong Phan, Hoa Nghiem, and Tri Hoang—and to Nicole Harrish who read my very first draft.

And Grant, thank you for cooking and cleaning and caring for our children, so that I could daydream and write.

FLOOD

Ma made a big mistake when she named me. In Vietnamese, my name, Yen, means calm or peacefulness. I was anything but. We had just finished supper, and I was in the middle of cleaning up when the sky grew suddenly dark. My heart dropped. I looked up at the heavens, and when I saw the black sky crack open, I shook like the earth beneath my feet.

Ma's shouts brought me back. "Grab Tien! Climb the ladder!"

The chopsticks fell from my hands. My heart skipped. *Where's Tien?* I whipped my head around the kitchen. She was nowhere to be seen. The river water was pouring in through the cracks of our house and rising quickly. Screams outside were muffled by the torrents of rain drumming on our rooftop. Thunder rumbled. Lightning flared. And in another flash, the rushing water was up to my knees.

Ma hollered again. "Yen, grab Tien! Climb the ladder! I'll get Quang."

I shuffled through the water with slow, weighted steps. The rain pounded, and I became conscious only of my own breathing—heavy and laboured. The room turned upside down and inside out. The current swept my feet from under me and my arms flung into the air. I grasped desperately for something to hang on to.

Our village was being washed away. We were being washed away.

The rushing water slammed me into a post. I gagged and coughed out a mouthful of muddy water and pulled myself back up onto my feet. My ears buzzed. Peering across the darkened house, I made out Ma's outline. She had one arm outstretched under the glow of a kerosene lamp held high above her head. She was barking at me, "Where is Tien?" Seeing that I had no answer, she jerked her head away and desperately searched the room.

The front door burst open. Our furniture floated into the raging Mekong. I was certain that we too would be dragged out to sea by the mighty river. I dug my heels into the dirt floor hoping to delay the inevitable.

I have to find Tien.

The flame in Ma's hand emitted enough light to cast shadows across the rush of water. Something was rising up from the swirling waters and bobbing toward me. It rolled over once, twice, and then bellied up. I dove.

"I have Tien, Ma!"

I whisked her up the ladder onto the loft. Tien coughed and sputtered and coughed some more, but refused to cry. Her wet hair was matted to her cheeks. There was an almost gleeful look on her face. I clung to her tightly.

We hung our heads over the edge of the loft looking for Ma. I followed her orange flicker of light. She found Quang at the far end of the hut, crouching on his bed, clinging to the mosquito net that dangled from the ceiling. In the dim light of Ma's lamp, I could see that his face had lost its colour.

"Hold on tight, Quang," I reassured from the loft. "Ma's coming!"

Quang shrieked when a corner of the net snapped from the ceiling. The strong current dragged his little feet to the edge of the wooden bed, which was now lifting off the ground. Quang cried louder than the day we found him abandoned on the side of the road four years before.

Ma finally reached him and draped him over her back like a bundle of sticks. She carried the whimpering load up to the safety of our loft. She then turned around and slid back down into the rushing water. I trembled and followed.

Nam Mô A Di Dà Phật. I place faith in Buddha. I prayed over and over while the thunder rumbled and the lightning crashed above our heads.

Ma prayed too. "The gods are angry," she said.

Nam Mô A Di Dà Phật, Nam Mô A Di Dà Phật, I repeated, my eyes sealed shut and palms tightly clasped against my chest. If my hands were closer to my heart, maybe the gods would spare us. The heavens exploded again like another thousand bombs detonating across the jungle. The gods have no mercy.

"Go to sleep, Yen," Ma said, clutching Tien as if we would lose her again to the river. Quang was sprawled by her other side, his chest rising and falling at a slow even pace.

Go to sleep? How can anyone sleep? The flood was about to swallow us, and the thatched roof might soon collapse from the pounding wind and rain. *How would our older sister and brother, Muoi and Lam, find us then? How would Ba know our fate?*

Before long, Ma too was asleep, Tien in her arms like a fragile newborn chick folded into her mother's wings. I wanted to shake Ma, to wake her. She needed to be up with me. *How could she pray for us when she was sleeping?*

Beyond the thatch walls, in the howling wind, our boat knocked and tapped against its mooring. We wouldn't drown if we were safely on it.

A white bolt of lightning lit up the loft. Long enough for me to see a puddle forming at our feet as rain dripped through a crack in the thatch roof. Long enough for me to see clearly the tiny space we had taken refuge in, long enough for the reality of our plight to soak in.

I sighed.

Where would we go when the sun had abandoned us? We were trapped by a cloak of darkness that descended from above and a river that raged from below.

My stomach growled as loud as the wind. There was no point waking Ma. I tossed myself over onto my other side. Of course Tien and Quang were sound asleep. They had eaten my share of rice at supper.

Another clap of thunder, and the house shook. My trousers were still drenched My eyes wandered around our loft. Ma's sewing machine, the sickle, hoe and other kitchen items were stacked against the sloped ceiling. We really didn't have much to salvage. At least we managed to save Ma's sewing machine. It was our lifeline.

"Close your eyes," Ma mumbled, drifting in and out of sleep. "There's much to do in the morning."

If we see morning, I thought bitterly. Certainly it was not a matter of if, but rather when, the river would drag us from our home. The only thing separating us from the floodwater below was the thin wooden floor of the loft. There was no point praying. No gods, Buddha or ancestors were coming to help us.

Tears welled in my eyes. I didn't want us to be crushed.

I didn't want us to drown. Ba would not find us then.

The sound of screams and panic from beyond had long faded, muted by the lashing wind. The other villagers must have been washed away, especially from homes without lofts like ours. Or else they made it to safety and had left us here all alone. Tears streamed down my cheeks like the pouring rain.

Tien woke abruptly with a frightful shrill. Quang slumbered on, unperturbed. I quickly wiped away my tears. I could not let Ma see me cry. With Muoi and Lam away, I was the big sister. Because I hadn't sprouted yet as tall as Muoi, I had to prove to Ma that I was just as wise. We had escaped the bombs, after all. I should have more courage.

"Ah, ahh," said Ma, rocking Tien to and fro. Then she started to sing a familiar tune:

> *The breeze pushes and sways,*
> *Back to the grove we shall go,*
> *Where the sweet coconuts and mangoes do*
> *grow,*
> *Back to the sea we shall go,*
> *To where the fishes in plenty swim,*
> *Back to the field we shall go,*
> *Where the rice and greens . . .*

In that moment, I couldn't resist closing my eyes. The folk song was as soothing then as it was when I was much younger, when Ma held me as she now held Tien. The melody made sweet honey from sour durians, every time. For just a moment, my restless thoughts found refuge.

MiST

My heart was thundering in my chest. I gasped desperately for air. Water flooded my lungs. As hard as I tried, I could not scream. The more I tried, the heavier my chest became. I flailed my arms frantically, but no one came. I sank deeper and deeper.

Just as I took what could have been my last breath, a blinding light ripped through the abyss. The weight upon my chest lifted. I recoiled and sheltered my eyes from the glare with the crook of my elbow. A pang of grief surged through me, and a mirage of faces lit up before my eyes. That was it.

I waited.

And waited . . .

But nothing happened.

A fiery heat was scorching my cheeks. I dared not open my eyes. Could being dragged through *tầng địa ngục*, as Ma called the eighteen levels of hell, be this painless? For all the sins I had committed in my life, it wouldn't surprise me to have been banished to the underworld for a thousand years. Ma often said that's where I'd go.

But rather than the piercing screams of tortured souls, upon my ears fell the ebb and flow of little breaths and a familiar kind of wet snort. Tien. Quang.

I realized then that the heat upon my cheeks was not from the wretched underworld but from the steam that rose from my own breath. I was dizzy with relief. I dropped my elbows and opened my eyes, lured by a ray of light beaming through a crack in the thatch roof. I squinted. It was daylight.

The storm had passed.

I took in a deep breath and my stomach unwound. It felt surreal to inhale full breaths of air. Until last night, I had seen only men, not gods, in their rampage. We must have angered the gods. But somehow the gods had failed to uproot our house.

A bamboo-green gecko was staring at me. It clung to the strips of palm that lined the rafters. My eyes narrowed to a slit to bring it into focus. It looked curious, probably frightened of my intentions. If I were Tien, the gecko would have much to fear. She would be chasing it to no end, to probe and prod and coddle in her tiny palms.

I was not fond of geckos, large or small. Ma said people used them as medicine. The sick would prop a gecko on their tongue and pinch its tail to send it scurrying down their throat. How would that cure anyone of their illness? I think people would just die swallowing something that crawled around inside them.

Quang stirred and clumsily slapped his bare foot on the hollow floor. The gecko scurried away. I lifted my head to check on Tien. She was lying sideways at my feet, spread out on her stomach. Her half-squished face lacked mischief in slumber.

Ma said children's spirits wander away to play during their sleep. I decided to let their spirits play for a while longer. We could have lost Tien last night if it weren't for *Mụ bà*, the Guardian Deity of Children, who swept her into my arms. Actually, if it weren't for *Mụ bà*, we would have lost Tien many moons ago. Last monsoon, we had to fish her out of the river, after she didn't listen to our warnings and played too close to the edge of the bank. Ma said it was *Mụ bà* who summoned the fish to keep Tien afloat long enough for us to find her. I wouldn't have had the same luck—at the age of thirteen, I was already too old for *Mụ bà*.

My stomach was twisted in a knot. The heavy air had settled in my lungs. It was like the morning after the Viet Cong army invaded and bombed Ca Mau—when all was shattered and silent, when at the break of dawn the roosters were not to be heard, and the songbirds did not sing. Though the air did not have the same burning smell of smoke or death, the loft was saturated with the same sour smell of destruction.

I took another look around the loft. Something was terribly wrong.

Ma was gone.

I bolted upright. Where could she have gone?

I got onto my hands and knees and started crawling, taking care not to brush against the little ones' legs. I paused when the floor creaked. The children snored and I exhaled.

Cautiously, I leaned over the edge of the loft, and gasped.

There was still water everywhere, extending to all four corners. Dark murky water halfway up our house. Where the front door had been was a large gaping hole. I could no longer see where the land ended and riverbank began. The remaining walls were in tatters. Palm shreds were strewn across the surface of the water. A chunky bamboo bed, too wide to escape, knocked against the walls.

Ma was nowhere to be seen.

"Ma," I whispered, hoping my voice carried across the water to wherever she was.

I waited, but received only silence in return.

We were stranded.

Was Ma swallowed by the river? I gave my head a shake to erase such awful nonsense.

Behind me erupted a loud squawk. "Mama!"

Startled, I whipped around to find Tien staring back at me with large puffy eyes and rosy cheeks. Her shoulder-length hair was a tangled mess.

Behind her, Quang unfolded from his deep sleep. He inched forward, his face a mix of confusion and worry. He always had a sad look, but this was something more.

"Mama?" Tien said again. Still no word from Ma.

I shook my head and shrugged my shoulders, but that was not a good enough answer for them.

"Stay here. I'll go find Ma."

As I stepped around onto the ladder, Tien lunged forward, pleading to come along.

"Stay back!" I snapped and pushed her away. "You want to drown?" Their stunned faces told me the words came out harsher than I had intended, but I needed to be firm. Neither of them knew how to swim. I knew because Lam had taught me. I wasn't very good, but at least I could float better than they could.

Without another word, Quang dragged Tien back from the edge and they retreated toward the corner. The slant of the thatch ceiling swallowed them in its shade.

On the last rung, I hesitated. My head would be above water, or at least I thought it would be. I shivered and stepped off the ladder. It was deeper than it looked. I had to tiptoe. The water was tepid and muddy.

My eyes widened as I waded through the mouth of our house into the grey open sky. Overnight, the fields behind our house had been transformed into a vast stagnant sea as far as my eyes could see. There were a few other huts in the distance that remained intact as ours did, with their ruffled thatch roofs rising just above the waterscape. Others had vanished completely into the night, leaving a haunting mist in their places. Scattered debris drifted past.

In the palm groves to the north of our hut, the partially submerged trees kept their beauty, while the clusters of banana trees peeked out meekly just above the dark waters.

Our boat was gone. Had the storm taken it too?

There were moving shapes and scattered voices in the distance. I didn't get far before a little wooden rowboat drew near. "Are you alright, child?" asked Cô Sáu, our neighbour to the east. Her lanky husband stood stoically with his oar and leaned over to offer me a hand up.

I was caught off guard by Cô Sáu's friendliness. I didn't know how to answer when she wasn't yelling at me. I had become good at evading her, an achievement in itself considering how near to us they lived.

I shook my head at the invitation to board. "I'm alright, Cậu Sáu," I said, avoiding eye contact with his wife. "But Ma is gone. Have you seen her?"

"No," Cô Sáu said, staring at the devastation. I was

standing where their house once stood. Only a broken corner pole jutting from the water marked the spot. "We've just returned from upriver. Everything is gone." Tears started pouring out of her and she wailed miserably. I regretted asking the question, though her tears came as no surprise.

"This is all we have left," Cô Sáu cried, her eyes hanging over the small bundle on her lap. A few strands of silver hair dangled across her sagging face. Cô Sáu made me nervous. Every word I had ever said to her had upset her in one way or another. Apparently it wasn't all my fault. Ma said it was because Cô and Cậu Sáu had owned a big trading company in Saigon, and the Viet Cong confiscated everything from them after the war. I didn't know if that would justify her brusque manners, but only Cậu Sáu had enough patience for her tantrums.

"What have we done in our past lives to deserve this?" she lamented.

I bit my tongue. I could easily think of ten things just in the past year of knowing them to account for this, but she wouldn't like me to speak of it. I felt sorry for Cậu Sáu though. His face was long, shoulders drooped, understandably defeated. I felt his loss.

Cô Sáu whimpered, "We've lost everything, we have nothing left."

Cậu Sáu stroked the water with the oar and propelled

them onward. Cô Sáu's whimpers trailed behind them. "What have we done to be punished so? What have we done?"

I watched as they paddled away, toward the rising sun, until they faded into the mist. Her words echoed in my head. I shuddered.

If only Ba were here. He would know how to repair things, to help us rebuild. The years away from him had already been much too long, and much too hard.

Trudging through the floodwater was slower and more tedious than I had anticipated, but I was half-expecting Ma to appear at any moment. I was relieved when Bác Minh's roof came into view. If anyone knew where Ma was, it would be Bác Minh. His home was nearby, but I had to be careful with the submerged tangles of branches.

If Bác Minh were gone too, I would be lost.

The tightness in my throat eased when I saw him. He too must have found refuge up in his loft. Alone on his boat, he now sat in front of his battered and partially submerged hut. His little wooden boat, not much longer than the width of his home, now loomed larger than the whole hut. Solemnly, Bác Minh sat in the morning sun, trying with tremulous hands to light an incense stick. Over and over he struck at a tiny matchbox pinched between his crooked fingers, but he was not successful.

"Let me help you, Bác Minh," I spoke up as I slid through the water. Bác Minh nodded and gestured for me to climb on. The water clung to me, but with the help of Bác Minh, I broke from its hold on the third heave and clambered on board without flipping over his boat.

The matchbox was a little damp, but with one brisk strike I set the little stick ablaze and proudly handed him the flame. I stared quietly as Bác Minh lifted the burning incense clasped between his palms to his forehead, mumbled a few words, then bowed to the heavens. He planted the incense in a small crevice at the bow of the boat and sat back, cross-legged, in silent contemplation. I chose to just watch. I didn't see the point of praying when it had made such little difference.

Bác Minh was elderly, but not so stooped for his age. Wispy white hair dangled from his chin. I had often delighted in seeing his toothless smile. I knew there was little in his lonesome life to smile about, but he always smiled and waved to us from the field, especially when I came straggling by with Tien, Quang and a tail of ducklings. I didn't know much about Bác Minh's life, but I understood from Ma that he had seen much through the Japanese, French and finally the American years of war and conflict in our Vietnam.

Though the soldiers had laid down their bullets and bombs three years ago after the tanks had pulled into

Saigon to liberate us—*giải phóng*, they called it—we weren't any more free or safe. Despite our prayers, the northern soldiers had taken everything from us in the years following *giải phóng*. Much the same way as the southern soldiers had taken Ba away before the so-called liberation to chew him up and spit him out.

"You are frowning, child," Bác Minh said. I tried to unknit my brows. Everything was still a blur in my mind. Our lives had changed so much after they had returned Ba. I was about ten, and Tien not even a year old, when we left him and slipped away into the night. Like lost spirits, we had been wandering across the Mekong delta, in search of what, I could not fathom. The whole countryside was painted with the same brush of dreariness.

"The waves come, the waves go," Bác Minh murmured. "The sun rises, then falls. Trees blossom, then wither . . ."

I sighed. Sometimes I would sit on the dusty path outside his house, doodling in the dirt with a stick, just to hear Bác Minh recite his poetry. Sometimes I even felt I knew more about the lives of the poets he named—who were arrested after *giải phóng* for words now deemed traitorous—than about him.

"Have you seen Ma, Bác Minh?"

Then, as if the wind had whispered secrets in his ear, Bác Minh lifted his head. His feathery white brows framed despair in his eyes as he pointed to something behind me.

I looked around, the cusp of my hands shading my eyes from the glare of the morning sun.

The silhouette of a woman standing on a boat appeared from the mist. With slow, delicate strokes of her oars, she steered deliberately toward us. The outline of her thin body was familiar. My heart rejoiced. *Ma!*

Where, and why, had she gone? But then it didn't matter. I was just glad the waves didn't rob us of her.

As the glare faded and light filled the darkness and shadows, my eyes became transfixed on something at her feet. It was the outline of something small. The outline of someone. It was a child, a small child, lying at Ma's feet. Motionless.

INCENSE

The child was dead.

A glimpse of his face made the sky and sea spiral. I knew him. It was Trinh, one of our neighbours down the river. He was about five, no older than Tien.

Ma told me to leave. I did not protest.

I slipped back into the water. My whole body trembled, my knees weakened. I had so little strength that if my knees had buckled, I might have drowned. But I had to go.

The water rippled as I pushed forward. I dared not look back.

I overheard Ma whispering to Bác Minh that she found only the one child. Trinh's older brother and sister were gone. The current had come to carry Trinh's siblings back to sea, back to their ancestors who lived by the sea.

Ma was working on her knees, fidgeting with the iron stove that we had dragged up from the floodwater the night before. I was slumped in the corner of the loft, a chill sweat beading on my forehead. My arms and legs were limp. I was sick to my stomach. I wanted to throw up, but I choked back the bile in my throat.

Tien and Quang were playing below. Their giggles were grating to my ears. It sounded like they were on the boat, splashing at the water with the oar.

Ma had a small pile of twigs and bark sitting on the floor by her feet. She must have gathered them in the morning as the broken branches drifted by. One by one, she twisted and snapped the wood into smaller pieces to feed the stove. Around the end of another stick, she wrapped a small piece of cloth, soaked it in a little kerosene, and lit it to entice the wood with its flames. It took a few nudges, but Ma persisted until the damp wood ignited.

Ma said not a word to me. Nor I to her.

The flickering and crackling of the flames was mesmerizing. As I stared, faces began to take shape in the fire. There were people crying and screaming, fear or desperation in their eyes. I had seen those faces many times before. I shut my eyes and hid my head under my arms, my knees tight against my chest.

Ma was too busy to notice me. Or maybe she just chose to ignore me. For a moment, I thought she glanced over at me, perhaps to check on me, but I was mistaken. She was just tilting her head to sweep a stray strand of hair that had fallen over her eyes. She carried on preparing the rice.

I expected nothing more; Ma had been hardened by the years away from Ba.

The aroma of freshly cooked rice brought torture and pleasure in every breath. The steam that rose from the clay pot delighted us. I salivated, ready to eat.

Ma said, "Light an incense."

What?! The sun was already high in the sky. I was sure the spirits would have understood if Ma fed her starving children first. The spirits were more than welcome to join us at the next meal.

Of course, when Tien and Quang looked to me to make the first move, I could not help but be the model big sister. We had to be grateful to Buddha and our ancestors, Ma said. But with the flood beneath us, our house in shreds and Ba gone, I saw little to be grateful for. I offered only half a bow. The children followed with more eager kowtows as the smoke from the burning incense encircled us, ascending softly and gracefully into the air.

"Don't grab so much," Ma said, slapping my wrist, the first words she uttered to me all morning since crossing paths at Bác Minh's. I jerked my hand back like a thief caught in the act. I hated having to wait just because I was the older sibling. It was a duty to yield to the younger children, Ma had often said. It was a duty to look out for them. I crossed my arms and stewed.

Tien was digging freely at the rice. Not fair. She had more to eat the day before. So had Quang, and he wasn't even blood.

I nibbled on the sticky rice residue on my fingers while Ma kneaded the small amount of rice we had into little balls and distributed them among us. We sat in a circle with nothing but the clay rice pot between us. It felt strange eating in the humid confines of the loft. As we chewed, we spat out grains of tiny rocks and sand that peppered the rice. I tracked the number of rice balls going around. I was shorted again!

I sighed. It didn't matter really. I couldn't eat much anyway. My gut was full with the weight of a hundred stones.

I wanted to cry.

Only a few short days ago, I was dangling from the nearby monkey bridge with Trinh and his siblings, the oldest being his sister, Mai. She was two years younger than me, and we played a lot together between looking after the little ones. The dusty path by Bác Minh's house was our favourite spot.

My head started to ache. Mai's sweet voice, Trinh's bubbly giggles, their brother's shouts and laughter reverberated through my head. I could see them—we were splashing in the rain, climbing up the mango trees and leaping through the air, as happy as if the

30

ravages of war were in a distant land.

How was it possible that Ma was saying prayers for their spirits? A sharp pang stabbed at my heart. Where was the guardian *Mụ bà*? Could this be a nightmare from which I would soon awaken?

I knew of many deaths from the bombings, the air raids and napalm that shredded and burned nearby villages and jungles, but until that morning, I hadn't seen the dead. Ma had meticulously shielded our young eyes from the bodies for fear we would lose our souls. I saw nothing, but I still could hear the high-pitched wails of neighbours finding their loved ones buried in the rubble. Or not finding them at all.

Now that I had laid eyes on the dead, I knew it was only a matter of time before they came to fetch *my* soul.

Ma had to nudge me a few times before I realized she had placed in my hand a piece of crusted rice from the bottom of the pot. I eagerly took a bite into its crunchiness. So Ma hadn't forgotten that this was my favourite part of the rice. Ma would say that it was a sin to waste rice, that your ancestors would eat maggots if you wasted rice. I smiled proudly as the last of the crust disappeared into my belly. Not one grain wasted.

"Bác Minh will look after the boy," Ma said.

I was caught off guard. Ma broached the topic so nonchalantly that I was confused. Quang and Tien were oblivious. Could Ma be suggesting that Trinh was still alive? Was it all really a bad dream?

"Trinh is going to be alright?" I asked.

Ma looked down at me with pity. With a flat expression betraying no emotions, she said, "Bác Minh and I said prayers for him and his siblings this morning. I've lit another incense for little Trinh. Their parents should be on their way back, maybe by sunset."

I couldn't bear looking at her. I had to turn away to hold back the tears. I didn't know which was worse, for Trinh's parents to make it through the storm to discover the devastating loss of not one but all their children, or for the children to lay waiting for all of eternity for their parents to return. Another stabbing pain pierced my chest. Perhaps it would have been better if their parents had perished too.

Ma had gone to their hut that morning because she and Bác Minh knew that Trinh's parents sailed regularly to the markets downriver while the children stayed home. We all had to make a living. Mai was more than capable of looking after her young brothers, but they did not have a loft. How could the parents have known that the gods would come to steal their children back out to sea?

As Ma diligently picked at the sides of the pot to ensure each grain of rice was eaten, something gnawed at me. And it gnawed at me until I blurted, "Can we go back to find Ba?" Ma's look went acid, and I knew it was too late to take it back.

"We don't need him," she said without looking back at me.

"But he can help us, Ma."

"You are no wiser. You foolish child."

"But he can fix—"

"Enough," she interrupted. Her eyes flashed with fury, firmly shutting me down. And that was the end of that.

I spent the rest of the day fuming. Why was Ma so difficult, irrational, obstinate? We needed Ba more than ever. Ba would protect us, I was sure of it.

There must be a way to get back to Ba in Ca Mau. If we could find him again, Ma would see that I was not so foolish after all.

The sun fell all too soon. I kept an eye out for Trinh's parents, but none of the shadows at dusk became them. My ears were peeled for their voices, but there were no cries for missing children. When we could sit no longer, I laid down, awake and waiting. Through a small hole in the east wall, I gazed out at the reflection of the moon, shimmering across the water. A million fireflies were in flight, dancing beneath the dark sky. The crickets sang and sang.

Quiet! I demanded.

While the others slept, I waited, not sure what I was waiting for, or whether I wanted to face whatever that was, but I kept waiting.

Until *they* came. I sprung up from the floor. My heart raced. Under the moonlight, two dark figures were gliding across the silvery water.

Ghosts!

"Ma!" I tried to scream, but no sound came from my throat. I choked.

Ghosts! I panicked. They're coming. They're coming to take my soul.

From afar, faint cries of a child drowned out the songs of the crickets. They too had seen the ghosts.

Closer and closer they came. Two figures, as frightening as the night.

PROVIDENCE

Lam craned his neck toward me and chuckled. "You thought we were ghosts?"

I felt my cheeks glow red like a rambutan, and it wasn't from the stove's heat. I crossed my arms and threw darts at him with my eyes. But then I sighed and looked away. As annoyed as I was at Lam for laughing at my expense, I was not going to waste another breath on the matter. At least my soul was still mine to keep.

"Never mind your brother. He'll forget last night soon enough," Muoi said as she produced something from behind her back.

I gasped. It was a brand new notebook! I could smell the crisp perfume of the handmade paper from across the loft, but I dared not presume that it was for me. I hesitated.

"It's for you, silly," Lam said. "Take it."

Delighted, I snapped the notebook from Muoi's hands. I was ready to tear open the pages when Ma said firmly, "We don't have money for you to waste."

I nodded and settled back in the corner to revel in its beauty. I wondered if Muoi and Lam had to work extra long hours after school at Tòa Cũ's crayon factory to buy the notebook. If it weren't for Tòa Cũ, who covered Muoi and Lam's high school tuition in Saigon, they would be out in the rice paddies with us. Tòa Cũ could afford to help them because he was a teacher by day and factory owner by night.

Tien took little interest in the gift. Instead, she draped herself over Muoi, twirling Muoi's long hair around her tiny fingers. Quang watched me open the notebook, wide-eyed. But then he looked down and pulled away. He wanted one for himself.

I was relieved when Muoi handed Quang a small box. "Crayons direct from uncle's factory," she said proudly. Quang grabbed it and laid down beside me, content with his newfound fortune. The notebook was mine.

Muoi turned back to huddle with Ma and Lam and finish up the morning rice. I lowered my head over the book. Its off-white pages felt like silk between my fingers. Images came alive in my head. I held tightly onto my pencil. It wanted to dance across the pages. I had to tame its energy. It was critical for me to think long and hard before I dared make a mark on the clean pages. Though Ma was immersed in conversation with Muoi and Lam, I knew there was a high probability that she had a long

36

measuring stick somewhere up her sleeve, ready to whip it out at any one of us if we were to waste paper. Ma was quick with the stick. Thankfully, Lam's buttocks were better acquainted with the stick than mine. I wondered if Tòa Cũ was as punishingly strict as Ma. I had my doubts. School teachers were more diplomatic.

From the corner of my eye, I saw Tien move. One minute she was innocent and sweet like an angel; the next, vicious and wild like a tiger. She pounced on Quang, clawing at the crayons. Quang pulled in his neck and arms like a turtle into its shell. He clung to his treasure.

"Mine!" Tien demanded. "I want them."

I was annoyed by their rowdiness. For two years after we had found Quang crying on the side of the road, he didn't speak. And now, he was a constant source of trouble. Ba had known he would be as soon as he saw Ma walking through the gate with Tien in one arm and Quang whimpering in the other. Things would have been different for us if we had never brought him home.

"No fighting," Ma declared. She reached over, pulled Tien off Quang and offered her a sip of boiled water from a hollowed-out coconut shell. "All you have is each other. Watch over one another." She wiped the sweat off Tien's forehead and released her back into the wild.

Quang let out a huff and rolled over to make room for Tien between us. Tien's eyes sparkled, and I shook my head. If it were me fighting with Muoi and Lam, Ma would have whipped me.

"How did you know about the flood?" Ma said to Muoi.

"I had a dream," Muoi confided. "Fire was raining down from the sky. A sea of blood. Tien was screaming inconsolably, crying out my name. The dream was so vivid that I woke up trembling. That's why we came home."

I swallowed hard and my ears popped.

"*Nam Mô A Di Dà Phật*," Ma praised. "Divine Providence." Lam and Muoi nodded in agreement. "You need to light an incense immediately and say a prayer," said Ma. "By the grace of Buddha and our ancestors, you made it home safely."

I scrunched up my nose. *Where was Buddha during the storm?* But I decided Divine Providence could be interpreted in many ways. Maybe Muoi and Lam had been summoned home for other reasons—perhaps to help take us back to Ba. Ba could help us out of this.

"It wasn't a good idea, coming in the storm," Ma said.

"The clouds were dark and the rain was steady in Saigon," said Lam, "but we had no idea it was this bad here. The wind and rain didn't pick up until we got on the boat in Bac Lieu. But I was steering."

"Pride is a foolish thing," Ma said. "By the grace of Buddha, the heavens cleared and the storm abated. Someone was watching over you."

Whatever the reason for their return, it was nice to have Muoi and Lam back. I would have a break from Ma's scrutiny and criticism. She still faulted me for Tien falling into the river last year. And she didn't like me asking about Ba.

Muoi's soft voice quivered when Ma asked about her marks. Her eyes watered. "I'm trying hard."

"Don't feel bad, Muoi. We are poor. You cannot expect to outperform students from wealthy homes. They have more opportunities."

"But I have done better than them, Ma. It isn't fair," Muoi insisted. "One of my classmates stole my assignment and put her name on it. She ended up getting top marks for it!"

"Crying won't help," Ma said. "Work harder next time to prove yourself. Always be wary of who you trust. There are always some people who will take advantage of you and try to keep you down. That kind of person thinks a poor girl shouldn't do better than a rich girl."

As they talked, I glided my pencil in grand cursive letters, like Muoi would write in her school notebooks. I wanted to write out the poetry that Bác Minh had recited, but my writing came out looking anything but graceful. Perhaps I could become a scholar and write as beautifully as Muoi if I went to school in Saigon with her and Lam, but I was needed here to help plough, harvest and thresh the rice, and to take care of the little ones while Ma sewed. Besides, at school in Saigon I would probably waste my time daydreaming.

The nearest middle school to our village was dozens of kilometres away, across deep channels, through heavy mangroves and muddy fields. "The world is your classroom," Ma would say to encourage me. I suppose sitting on the dusty road listening to Bác Minh's poetry was like sitting in class. For all the homeschooling Ma had given us, she couldn't hide the fact that she could barely read or write herself. What few skills she had were from having eavesdropped on her brothers' lessons in her younger years. Bà Ngoại, Ma's Ma, saw little value in girls going to school. There was work to be done around the home. "This is my lot in life," Ma would say sometimes, with a sigh, when she thought she was alone, tending to the bleeding cracks in her heels and hands.

Trinh's name fell from Lam's lips and a veil of melancholy shrouded the loft. I shifted uncomfortably and wanted to cover my ears, but didn't. I wanted to know if Trinh's parents had returned. But Tien was squabbling with Quang again over the crayons, and the discussion became increasingly difficult to hear.

"Quang, Tien, stop your arguing!" I hollered. But they went on nattering back and forth just the same. Frustrated, I sat upright and turned to face Ma, expecting a united front against the squawking children. Instead my stomach knotted, seeing the looks on their faces. Something was wrong.

Muoi said, "Tòa Cũ says we should escape with him."

"Quang!" I shouted. "Look what you did!"

Quang had knocked over the coconut shell, spilling its contents over the pages of my notebook. I must have had a shocked look on my face, because he withdrew in horror. I knew it was an accident and that it was just as much Tien's fault as Quang's, but I couldn't control myself. I yelled at Quang again. "You've ruined my book!"

Quang pulled back, wide-eyed. Seeing his white face made me burst into tears. Trinh's face flashed before me. I lost composure and sobbed uncontrollably, like a child. A flurry of questions filled my mind. *Escape? Escape from what? To where? What were they talking about?*

Lam quickly separated Quang from me while Ma grabbed the notebook from my hands to dab the pages dry with her shirt. The words I had drawn on its pages were smeared and ruined. I didn't want to leave.

"Stop your crying," Ma said. "You are not a child."

I bawled even louder.

Usually Ma would punish me for sure, but with Muoi home I wailed without fear. Muoi did what she always did. She stepped in between Ma and me and folded me into her arms. I knew I was safe. On and on I snivelled, to spite Ma.

At that moment, a hoarse throaty voice rippled through the shreds of thatched wall on the west side. I cut short the tears. Ma quickly swept the loose hair behind her ears and smoothed over her white top, embarrassed by the commotion.

"Huong?" the voice called to Ma. Peeking timidly through one of the holes in the west wall was Cô Lien, one of our neighbours, crouched on her boat. Her oily hair was pulled back in a bun, her leathery skin hidden in the shadows, and a bulging growth on the lower half of her neck protruded more noticeably than ever. Cô Lien's husband was a fisherman who fished the open seas. It was a habit of hers to stop by our place to tell us about his catches. Cô Lien once told of times when the fish and shrimp swam in abundance into his net, but lately they were scarce no matter where he searched. It was not a good year.

"Huong, would you be so kind as to lend us a cup of rice?" Cô Lien asked, reaching an arm through the hole. She held out an empty can in her hand. "We have lost so much in the storm. Our roof is barely holding up."

I shook my head. We hardly had enough rice for ourselves. If it weren't for Tòa Cũ, we would still be wandering from place to place to make a living. Knowing that we were on our own, Tòa Cũ reached out to Ma last year and offered to pay for Muoi and Lam's schooling in Saigon. As a teacher, it was hard for him to not see, at least the older kids, in school. In return, Ma agreed to care for this small piece of land in the delta, where the river twisted and bent and branched as the silky water flowed through the mangroves.

Even out here though, there was no escaping the Viet Cong officials. They requisitioned the grain we harvested to feed the people. Or so they said. They paid us farmers a sum so paltry that we had no choice but to give them most of our crop, leaving little for ourselves. With the flood, who knew if we would get any rations. As friendly as Cô Lien was whenever she visited, she never once offered us any fish, even knowing how hard things had been for us. Ma always had to scrounge for money to purchase even a few grams of shrimp from them.

But before I had even finished my thought, Ma had already invited Cô Lien to pull her boat into our house, up to the ladder. Ma proceeded to pour three scoops of rice into her can from our virtually barren rice bag. I stared in disbelief. I could tell Muoi wasn't too pleased either. Ma was going against all reason.

While she waited in her boat, Cô Lien said, "It must be nice to have Lam and Muoi home. What brings them back?" Ma did not say. So Cô Lien continued. "Our boys have been gone too long." Her two sons were in Bac Lieu, a town between Ca Mau and Saigon. Ma placed the can gently back in Cô Lien's hands. "We will bring you a big catch one day soon," she said, thanking Ma.

I scoffed at her words. I would believe it when I saw it.

"Not to worry, Lien," Ma said. "Save your earnings for your sons' school fees."

Or for a doctor, I thought, because the swollen mass on her neck was very distracting. I made an effort to keep my eyes on her eyes so I wouldn't be caught staring at her neck.

Cô Lien thanked Ma profusely and graciously bowed as she pulled away. I didn't know what to say. *Why would Ma give away so much rice when we had almost finished our ration for the month?*

"Bring this to Bác Minh," Ma tapped me on the head with another container. It was a rusty canister filled with rice. *Would there be any left for us?* "He must be running low too. Your notebook will be dry by the time you get back."

Relieved that Ma had forgiven my hysterics, I prepared to go. But Tien rushed over, squeezing her short little arms around my waist. I fell back and smiled at her. She squeezed tighter and I realized she was apologizing for causing all the ruckus. A weight lifted from my shoulders and, when I could finally get out of her embrace, I slid down onto our boat and paddled out into the open.

I welcomed the fresh air. But as I made my way to Bác Minh's house, my chest grew tight. I remembered the last time I had been there. My heart hammered against my chest. Like a nightmare being relived, the moment Ma glided out from the mist with Trinh's body flashed before me. I felt sick. I regretted accepting Ma's order to come here.

I stopped at a distance, out in the open where the sunlight harboured no ghosts. The air was humid and I felt faint.

"B-Bác M-M-Minh?" I called out.

No answer.

I refused to look inside. I took a deep breath and said, "Bác Minh, Ma sent some rice for you."

Still no sign of him. Anywhere. I decided not to linger another minute. I didn't want to find out where he had taken little Trinh.

I jabbed the oar into the ground to turn the bow of the boat around. Ma couldn't get upset with me when it wasn't my fault that he wasn't home. Just as I started to paddle, the cries of a child pierced the air.

I gasped and straightened up to listen.

The pitch was familiar. I recognized it. It was the same cry as from the night before. I spun my head all around. *Was it Trinh crying for his parents?* The noise was not coming from the darkness within Bác Minh's house. It came from some place beyond.

The nose of the boat drifted in the water toward the sound, as if with a life of its own. I gulped.

The water glittered like jewels in the afternoon sun, between rows of half-submerged palms plastered like paintings against the grey sky. High in the trees, a small brown monkey scurried by and dove into the foliage. The leaves rustled.

The hair on my arms stood on end, the cries grew louder.

Nestled in between large dark fronds of palm was a lonely little wooden house on stilts that rose above the floodwater. The relentless cries wrenched at my gut. I stood quietly, listening as the river coursed southward beyond the bend.

"That's enough!" a woman said. "I have shredded these bananas for you. Why won't you eat?"

Something slammed onto the floor and rolled a short distance. The squeal became unbearable. "Now you have nothing to eat! It's all we have!" the woman shouted.

The wooden floor creaked. I moved up to the window. The young mother was pacing back and forth in her loft, straddling a small boy on her hip. Her belly was round with another. The older sister was on the floor, red-faced.

To the young boy, the mother said, "There, there, my child, your daddy should be home any day now." When she turned around, I ducked below the window, uncertain if I wanted to be seen. "When daddy gets home, we'll have treats for you both. Rice and fruits and candies. Lots to eat." The mother wept. "Mama will feed you, my little ones."

The older sister did not want to listen, and screamed even louder against her mother's assurances. "Hungry! Hungry!"

"Stop it, I tell you!" the mother snapped. She dropped to her knees, released the little boy from her arms and firmly grabbed his older sister by the shoulders. "Do you want another spanking?" The child would not stop.

I pushed the boat up to their door. "Please, Cô!" I called out through the window. "If I may, Cô?" The crying came to a sudden stop.

"Who's there?" the young mother asked.

"My apologies, Cô. I am the daughter of Huong." She nodded. "Ma wanted me to bring this rice for your family. She thought you would need some because of the flood."

Her lips quivered. She struggled to contain herself. She did not say a word as she received the canister, but her eyes spoke enough to me. She retreated, canister in hand, and climbed back up their loft.

The young daughter peeked over the edge with her large brown eyes. She smiled at me and I smiled back.

I decided not to tell Ma that I had given the rice away to someone else. She did not need more reasons to punish me. But when I got home, Ma did not pay me any attention. Quang crawled up to me timidly and presented the notebook, all pressed and dried.

"It's good now," he whispered.

I smiled. "It's all good," I said, and his face lit up. I gave him a hug.

I couldn't help but notice a renewed energy in the room. At the other end of the loft, Ma, Muoi and Lam were planning a trip downriver to Ca Mau.

"We need to get more rice and supplies," Ma said.

"Ca Mau?" I asked. We hadn't been back to Ca Mau since we stole away three years ago, just months before *giải phóng*. Ma had not even mentioned Ca Mau since then. *What had changed?* It was unusual for her to choose Ca Mau when there were other closer markets, although they were much smaller.

Then I remembered: Ba was in Ca Mau. I wanted to go to Ca Mau too.

"I am going with you," I announced.

This was Divine Providence.

RIVER

Muoi didn't like crowds. She was soft-spoken and hated bartering. Where she thrived was in the classroom, not the markets, so it was obvious that I would be the better choice to go downriver with Ma. It was not unusual for me to be at the market while Muoi was at school, or at home at the sewing machine, like Ma.

While I attended to the kids, making sure Tien would not fall off the loft, Muoi and Ma muttered back and forth, taking stock of what we had salvaged from the flood. Ma said something about needing to sell these items to get enough money. "For food," she said, but I wasn't entirely convinced.

All the more reason for me to get back to Ca Mau, I decided.

Besides, I was fed up spending every day up in the loft. It wasn't particularly exciting to watch the floodwater retreat. Many tedious days and nights would pass before we could set foot on dry land again. There was barely enough room for all of us to stretch out our legs, especially at night when Tien rolled and kicked everything and everyone around her. During the day, there was not enough space for the children to play, and the heat outside was unbearable. Tien could only catch geckos and draw flowers in the air, and Quang could only make animal drawings or splash at the water for so long before their paths crossed and clashed.

By the fifth sunrise, Ma and I were ready to set out. An incense was burning in the urn even before the first light of day. We moved gingerly around Tien and Quang while they slept, but made haste to ensure that we were set for the journey. Muoi and Lam would stay back with the kids. Ma gave Muoi instructions on the outfits that needed tailoring while Lam waded through the water behind our house to gather bundles of bananas we would take to the market.

When he came back, he lifted a bamboo basket, tied to the ladder, out of the water. Noisy little critters clawed from within. Lam uncovered the lid for me to see, and I smiled. They were freshwater crabs that Lam was able to purchase from a nearby farmer. Ma knew we could fetch a good price for them in Ca Mau.

I sat quietly in the dim light, trying not to get in the way until I was needed. Ma said very little about the journey, but Muoi and Lam seemed to move with purpose, as if they already knew. Of course they knew. Muoi and Lam were the ones relaying Tòa Cũ's message to Ma. They just didn't care to fill me in on what they meant by "escape." That was fine, I had my own reason for going to Ca Mau, and if I was successful they would surely be proud of me.

When Muoi reached down from the loft to pass Ma the roll of steamed rice she had wrapped in banana leaves, I knew it was my chance to speak. With Ma preoccupied on the boat below, I leaned over, cupped my hand around Muoi's ear and whispered. "Ba is still in Ca Mau, right?"

Muoi pulled back with a jerk as if I had bitten her. I gulped. She knitted her brows and glared into my eyes, like she was trying to peer into my soul. The faint scar at the tip of her nose was now a deep visible crater because she was so close.

"Are you coming, Yen?" Ma called from below.

I did not answer.

"Why would you ask about him?" Muoi shot back, under her breath.

I shook my head. I didn't know why she was asking.

"Don't be foolish. It doesn't matter where he is. Don't you remember? He is of no consequence to us," she answered, jaw clenched. "Your duty is only to Ma." She hustled me down the ladder, onto the boat, and dropped the warped notebook and pencil onto my lap. I sat down, indignant, and crossed my arms angrily. With the baskets filled with a few household items, bundles of bananas, and freshwater crab at my feet, Ma steered our boat out of our living quarters and into the light of dawn.

Muoi and Lam, in their own boat, followed us out. Muoi made certain, when I glanced back, that I saw her disapproving scowl under the orange glow of the rising sun. With her flaming eyes, she issued a threat. If I made trouble, she was not going to stand between me and Ma's stick! I glared back at her and turned away, my nose pointed high in the air.

I didn't need Muoi's help anyway.

I forgot about my anger toward Muoi when we approached Bác Minh's house. Sadness crept over me instead, seeing him sitting wrapped in darkness on his boat. He was in mourning.

I wondered where he had gone with Trinh, but I did not ask. I did not want to know. Where could one be laid to rest with water stretching to the horizon? They say the spirits do not wander far from home.

He and Ma nodded politely to each other as we rowed on by.

There were many more boats, big and small, on the water that early morning, as if the Mekong River only became active when it spilled across the land. Some boats had a canopy, others had a little cabin, some were motorized and others, like ours, were mere rowboats, driven across the water by long wooden oars.

I sat cross-legged at the bow of our boat, with my fingers dipped in the water, as Ma stood tall at the stern propelling us forward. The two oars knocked gently on the sides as they rose and fell into the water.

For a good long time, I watched the curves of the ripples roll and change in shape, fanning out from my fingers in the water. When we passed the scattered stilt huts marking the sides of the river bank, I watched the people repairing the damages caused by the storm. Others bathed in the coolness of the river, and many others just sat in their boats, staring emptily at the people passing by.

Ma did not look back to meet their eyes. She never did. "Trust no one," she said. It was hard advice to refute when neighbours that we thought we knew turned out to be informants. That was how Ba came to be taken away.

I glanced at Ma in between strokes to see if she wanted to rest, but she showed no signs of exhaustion. We needed to get to Phong Thanh, a neighbouring village, and hire a motorized vessel to get us to Ca Mau before the sun peaked. Ma stopped rowing from time to time to wipe the sweat off her forehead, or to scoop handfuls of water from the river to cool down. She spoke little, even when I offered to help with the rowing.

"Just focus on your writing," she told me, hands firmly wrapped around the handles of the oars. Her tall, slender silhouette under her conical hat was strict and rigid, unfazed by the heat. "People can take everything away from you," she began.

"But they cannot take away your education," I completed the saying.

I looked down at the notebook on my lap. Its pages were crumpled, but usable. When I flipped it open, there, in colourful wax, was a scribbled drawing of our family, the six of us in stick shapes. Courtesy of Tien and Quang. I smiled.

I wondered if Ma truly believed her own words. At the end of the day, we all ended up doing the same thing, struggling to survive, on the same dusty road.

A chill suddenly came over me, and I woke from my wandering thoughts. We were going through a narrow passage with huge palms reaching high over our heads on both sides. A pair of small yellow birds fluttered by to kiss the water, then disappeared into the sunlight. Layers and layers of fronds crested to meet in the middle, forming a tunnel where the rays of the sun were blocked.

I trembled as we glided through this tunnel. Beyond the thick tangle of mangroves that lined the edges of the water, I caught glimpses of half a dozen brown sacs hanging from branches. They looked like butterfly cocoons, but without the beauty. Instead, I thought about the delicate curves of Trinh's face in eternal sleep.

"Turn your eyes away," Ma said. I could feel the strokes of the oars hastening, and I held my breath.

I looked down at my feet but Trinh's face kept flashing before me. I felt a little hand brush across my shoulders. I turned quickly to see, but there was no one behind me. Then little giggles, faint but near. My heart was beating harder, and I shivered. There were whispers coming from the shadows, but I couldn't look into the depths of the wood. Were the ghosts coming to steal my soul?

Despite Ma's rapid paddling, it felt like forever before the warmth of the sun once again touched my cheeks. When we were a good distance from the darkness and whispers, Ma's shoulders dropped and she finally sat down. She leaned over the water and splashed her face. I did the same on the other side. Ma said nothing, but I knew what was inside those sacks. Peace for them would not come until the sky once again touched the earth.

I offered her a sip of water from our bottle. I then offered the steamed rice wrap, but she declined. "Go ahead, you eat first."

Without hesitation, I unwrapped the roll and took a pinch. I looked around and savoured the quiet moment, in the middle of the calm stretch of river.

I had many questions about this trip. "Why Ca Mau?"

"Business," she replied tersely.

I didn't like the word "business." Ba left one morning supposedly on business too, but he never returned. I had tailed Ma to every corner of Ca Mau looking for him, but he was nowhere to be found.

"What kind of business, Ma?"

Silence.

"Will we be visiting anyone?"

"Likely." She shifted uneasily.

Silence yet again. I grew impatient.

"Who, Ma? Why won't you tell me?"

More silence. I wanted to scream from the top of my lungs that I was old enough to know these things, but I held my tongue. Children should never raise their voices to their parents and elders. One must always show respect and honour, they say.

Then Ma said, "Some relatives and old friends." She paused. "You ask too many questions." She wiped the sweat off her forehead, stood up and began rowing again. It was her signal to stop asking questions.

I missed Ba. He was different. I couldn't remember a time when he scolded me.

The further we travelled, the louder the world grew. The air became saturated with the sounds of motorized boats and wooden barges sputtering past us, some with small loads of fruits, timber or junk metal, others with nothing at all. The sullen faces of the men on board were distant and resigned. The smell of diesel exhaust was nauseating.

"Coconut milk here! Coconut!" chanted a short old woman who gravitated toward us as soon as we came around a narrow bend into the open water. "Coconut milk. Coconut! Who wants coconuts?"

I salivated. As the woman neared, I looked over to Ma, but she shook her head. I turned to the old woman and said, "No thank you, *Bác*. We are not interested."

The old woman smiled crookedly. "Ah, but you are. You are thirsty from the long journey. You have miles to go."

"We do not want to buy any," Ma repeated.

But the old woman either could not hear or would not listen. She pulled up next to us and proceeded to rummage through her pile of young green coconuts. She picked up one to inspect, shook it in her ear, then selected another as if the bright shell of this other one had my name written on it. We were compelled to watch her. With unusual precision and strength for her age, she sliced off the cap from the coconut using a rusty old machete and offered the coconut to me.

Ma held up her hand to dismiss her, but she refused to withdraw her offer until I took it. Ma did not stop me from doing so. The old woman smiled with a twinkle in her eyes, cupped her wrinkled hands and waited patiently for payment. I did not dare inhale even the scent of the sweet juice without Ma's consent.

Ma sighed, then reached into her pocket and pulled out a small bill and slipped it quickly into the old woman's hands. Ma must have given the woman more than what the coconut was worth, because the old woman lit up with a wide shiny grin that filled her eyes. A row of decayed teeth made the grin a little skewed.

Then she glided on her way, chanting loudly to the other river merchants. "Coconut milk, fresh coconuts for sale!"

The sweet juice vanished down my throat in one long gulp. I caught a rare glimpse of Ma smiling before she propelled us onward. With the sleeves of my shirt, I wiped the sweet milk from my lips, and smiled.

We found a spot to tie up our boat and hired a driver to take us down the last long stretch to Ca Mau.

MARKET

Ca Mau was much like I remembered, but the river that once bustled with diesel boats and people motoring in all directions seemed more subdued. The air was still heavy though with the smell of fish and garbage tossed into the river.

It took some time for the driver to steer his way through the tangles of the small floating market to dock. As our boat pulled up to the banks, two men stepped forward. They had dark stern looks and military-green uniforms. The taller one, with pitted acne scars on his cheeks, leaned forward and stopped us. His uniform cap cast a shadow over his dark eyes.

"What do we have here?" he asked. He stepped on the driver's hand as he was tying up the boat to the wooden dock, pinning him to the ground with his hard heel.

The driver winced in pain, but did not pull back or speak up.

The official crossed his arms, and with eyes narrowed

to a slit, gazed suspiciously down at us. I diverted my eyes, but Ma stared right back.

"We only have some food to sell at the market," Ma answered. She grabbed the driver's arm and pulled his hand from under the officer's foot. Then she handed the rope back to the driver. She had dealt with men like this before.

The second official shifted on his feet, uneasy at Ma's defiance. Taken aback and clearly offended, the pitted-face officer said, "I haven't seen you around here before."

"Why would you? We left Ca Mau years ago." She turned her back to them and pulled me out of the rocking boat.

"Where are your papers?" he demanded impatiently.

Ma pulled out our documents. We could go nowhere without our identification papers. The pitted-face officer scanned them and furrowed his brows. "*Người hoa*," he muttered with disdain.

Yes, we were *người hoa*. That meant we had Chinese ancestry. My brows furrowed too. *Were we not Vietnamese?*

"We have to inspect."

My heart started pounding. There was nothing to hide, but nonetheless I felt certain they would find something to fault because the papers identified us as *người hoa*. The driver retreated to the back of the boat to tend to his hand.

"There's nothing to inspect," Ma lifted the baskets

onto the dock and stepped up beside me.

The pitted-face official grabbed Ma's elbow to stop her. My breath caught in my throat. From the corners of his thin lips, he muttered, "Traitors will be punished." Ba had suffered at the hands of these uniforms. They were capable of ugly things, but Ma would not be intimidated.

She shrugged him off. "Excuse me, officer, I have children to feed," Ma said without looking back. She slid the carrying rod through the loops of the baskets and lifted them up onto her shoulders. I clung to her arm.

But the pitted-face officer would not let up. He and his companion stepped around us and blocked our path, their faces menacing. A couple of years before, when Ma and I had encountered some green uniforms stationed along a remote stretch of the river, they had worn the same menacing faces. They had used their badges to stop us, then confiscated all our merchandise.

Ma took in a deep exasperated breath and slapped some cash into the hands of the officer with the pitted scars. That was enough to appease them, and we made distance between us and them. *Thieves!* I scowled at them as we marched off.

We weaved cautiously through the crowds on the way to the market, hopping over rubble and garbage. It felt good to be surrounded by so many people, young and old.

I struggled to keep pace with Ma, her long legs nimbly leaping over ditches and down passages that were familiar to her. I dodged along, avoiding being knocked over by several rickshaws, only to be tripped by a one-legged man. I fell over.

Ma picked me up and dusted me off, profusely apologizing for my carelessness. He shook it off and, with his walking stick, pleasantly skipped away.

That was when Ma stopped and stared at an official-looking building with a soldier standing in front. Ma hesitated, and took a step back.

"Follow me," she said. I hesitated too, but followed her inside. This was not going to go over well.

Two large fans were spinning full blast from the ceiling. It was a welcome relief from the scorching heat outside. A red flag with a yellow star hung prominently on the centre wall. My knees knocked against each other. The uniformed men behind their desks stopped and stared at us. At the far wall sat a burly man who looked like he could be a senior official. He had a square jaw and bushy brows under neatly coiffed hair. Without blinking he stared us down, eyes full of scorn.

I tugged at Ma's sleeve, but Ma was not about to be dissuaded. She had waited years to do this. Because of them, we were left with deep financial debts to friends and relatives. We had been on the move, wandering from place to place, in an effort to rebuild and repay our loans. It had not been easy for Ma with us in tow.

"Your men have no compassion," she said.

He laid down the folder in his hand, rested his elbows on the desk and locked his fingers together.

"You must be in the wrong place," he said.

Ma ignored him and continued. "Your officer with the pitted scars is nothing more than a common thief."

The burly official stared at Ma with a blank expression.

"Just because your soldiers have won the war does not give them the right to oppress our people. Do you have no compassion? I have five young children to feed. If you want us to follow your rules, then you should act with a measure of principle."

With that, we flew out the door and hastened away with our baskets before he had a chance to react. The hot muggy air assaulted my lungs. It was suffocating, but I felt exhilarated.

The sun was almost at its peak by the time we arrived at the Ca Mau central market. To our dismay, it had been partially torn down and many of the vendors had been forced to sell their wares outside under rows of umbrellas. Still, for a brief moment, the sights, smells and sounds of Ca Mau market made me feel like I was five years old again, tagging behind Ba, hoping he would buy me treats.

But reality soon set in. The atmosphere of the market was more subdued than I remembered it being. Usually, we could find almost anything at the market, but now there were few things on display. Even the noise of buyers and vendors haggling back and forth was restrained.

We needed to find ourselves a spot to sell our stuff, but the rows of tables for produce and meat were occupied. With only a few customers, the meat vendors were busy chatting with each other, fanning their dangling strips of raw meat to keep away the flies. The tubs of shrimp, fish and eel stunk.

My mouth watered as we walked by the sparse but colourful display of mangoes, papayas, ambarella, yams and cassava. There was no room for us there.

We left the shaded corner and were back in the scorching heat. Though not as many vendors were out in the sun, the hardy ones, sheltered by their conical hats, had staked their grounds and spread their products out at their feet. There were myriads of items, from cans of roasted peanuts to *bánh xèo* and fried bananas, but few customers. A lady with toy windmills stretched her arm to hand me one, but Ma shook her head. We were not there to buy, Ma reminded me. A brown hen clucked and scampered between my legs. A little boy dashed by in pursuit and disappeared into the crowd.

A thin woman with hair pulled back in a loose bun

waved us over and made room for us next to her. She was selling a handful of dried shrimp. Ma bowed gratefully.

"Why are you here so late?" asked the shrimp lady. "You've missed the morning crowd." She chatted without giving Ma a chance to respond. "You look familiar. Have you been here before? What are you selling?"

Ma shook her head then nodded courteously. "It's been a few years. I don't think we've met."

I was eager to see the crawly crabs, but when Ma lifted the lid and looked in the basket, her face sagged. My heart sank. There was no movement inside. The tiny crabs had succumbed to the heat.

"Oh, what a pity," the shrimp lady said. I wanted to cry. I could sense that Ma wanted to burst into tears too, but she didn't, and so I didn't. One business venture after the other had turned sour, again and again. Ma thought we could make some money on this, but in the end, Lam's efforts to find the crabs were all for naught. The gods' favour had eluded us despite the burning of the incense.

A feeling of guilt washed over me. I had wasted money on the coconut milk.

Ma looked defeated, but she turned to me and said, "We won't sell anything with you just sitting there." I didn't appreciate her tone. I huffed and stewed and stared into the crowd. I resented Ma ordering me around. Muoi never got ordered around at my age.

"Go on, child, you haven't got all day," the shrimp lady urged.

I picked myself up and shouted, with vigour, "Bananas here! Fresh bananas! Crabs here! Fresh crabs for sale." It felt good shouting. I had learned a thing or two over the years about half-truths. It was a necessary survival skill. I repeated my chanting, over and over, and waited. And waited. But no one seemed interested. I watched as shoppers, many of whom were clad in black slacks and white *áo bà ba*, criss-crossed in front of us without even looking our way. Ma tried to engage them too, but without luck.

A yellow-uniformed official marched toward us.

"Police officers. They're in cahoots with the northern army. They take everything from us and send it to their friends and families," bemoaned the shrimp lady. "Have your vendor permit ready in case he checks." Ma leaned in closer to the shrimp lady. We had no permits to be there. To our relief, he passed us by. While Ma and the shrimp lady whispered back and forth, a woman stood over me. I could only see the darkened contours of her face in the shadow of the sun.

"Let me see the crabs," she said.

I lifted the lid. From behind her, the same little boy who was chasing the brown hen leaned forward. He was about the same age as Tien. His face was smeared with dirt, and highlighted his dark round eyes.

"They are still good, *Cô*," I said of the lifeless creatures.

The lady picked one up, but reflexively dropped it. "Why are you selling dead crabs?" she asked, rubbing her hands on her trousers. "Come." She signalled for the little boy to move on with her, but he didn't.

I smiled and asked him, "Do you want to see one?"

He nodded eagerly and smiled.

"Do you want to hold one?"

He bounced more enthusiastically. I held one out for him. Ma didn't pay me any attention. The little boy giggled as he took the little critter from my hands. I smiled at the way his plump cheeks jiggled.

"Let's go, Hoang." The haughty lady leapt back to swoop the child away.

I watched her march him around the dilapidated market building, her bag full from other purchases.

"Never mind her," said the shrimp lady. "She always acts like she's better than the rest of us here. She needs to look in the mirror." She then swivelled around and drew my attention in the opposite direction. "Look at that poor woman. Here she comes again." She pointed to a woman in a dusky blue *áo bà ba*. "She has been coming around every day, begging. A pretty woman too. What a shame."

I watched her as she roamed through the market, bouncing from person to person, her palms stretched out but receiving little in return. People passed by her like she was invisible. I caught a glimpse of her profile in the crowd. There was something familiar about her.

"Cô Sáu!" I called out.

She wrenched her head my way, and when she saw me, she blushed. It was indeed Cô Sáu. Ma hurried over to her and they embraced. Cô Sáu broke down in tears. The shrimp lady was speechless, for once. The women around us shifted over to make room for Cô Sáu to sit beside us. Ma offered her the last of our rice.

Cô Sáu wept as she voraciously ate what was left in our banana wrap. And as she wept she recounted how she and Cậu Sáu had come to Ca Mau looking for an old friend, but the friend and his family had disappeared.

Disappeared? What does that mean? I wanted to ask, but I didn't want to interrupt. Cô Sáu was explaining how, with nowhere to go and knowing no one else in Ca Mau, they had been sleeping in an abandoned alley. They dared not go back to Saigon. The soldiers there had confiscated everything they had.

"I know people who might be able to help you," Ma said. Cô Sáu looked so fragile with her shrunken frame, her hair streaked with strands of silver, that she seemed gentler. I met her eyes and felt her pain and loss.

Ma left me in charge of the baskets. While some vendors had already packed up and left, I was to stay and sell everything. Ma wanted to take Cô and Cậu Sau to find shelter. We had some relatives and old friends in Ca Mau.

"And watch your pocket," Ma said, leaving a few *đồng* bills in my pocket for change.

I rolled my eyes. She didn't need to remind me about pickpockets. I knew how to guard against them.

"Wait for me here."

I nodded. Of course I would, I told her.

"Don't wander off."

I nodded. "I won't."

But I knew what I had to do and where I had to be, and it wasn't in the market. As soon as Ma left, I turned and ran the opposite way.

"Where are you going?" the shrimp lady said as I ran off. "You'll get a whipping."

"I'm going to get help," I called back.

Ma had turned left. I went right.

"What about your baskets?" the shrimp lady yelled after me.

"Watch them. I'll be back in no time."

I bolted through the narrow streets. Storefronts lined the bombed-out and broken roads. Some of the stores that had crumbled under the bombs still sat in piles of rubble.

My heart thumped against my chest. There it was, as I remembered: the house with green-and-yellow striped awning where we had once lived.

The front quarter was now a hair salon. Luckily, the salon was empty. To the right, in front of the next house, was a lady selling small loaves of bread; to the left was a small *Phở* noodle house with knee-high red plastic tables. A shaggy-haired man was working at the corner across the street, repairing broken bicycles. No one was looking at me.

I swallowed and stepped inside.

There he was. Asleep.

SALLOW

"Ba! Ba!" I rushed to him. He was late coming home, but it didn't matter. He had been out chopping wood, and when he swept me up in his arms, I could smell his salty sweat. Ba held out a pink popsicle stick for me.

I grabbed it and scrambled away to the back of the house to devour it before Muoi or Lam could catch me with it. I was only five or six.

In the dim light, Ba looked just like I pictured him. I wanted to jump into his arms like I had done that day, but my feet were glued firmly to the ground. I was taller now, maybe even skinnier. My hair was definitely longer. He might not even recognize me.

"Where is the money I gave you?" I overheard
Ma whispering one early morning.

Ba was shaking his head as I tailed
Muoi and Lam into the kitchen and sat
down between them. They stopped mid-
conversation and turned to us. I beamed
when Ba scooped a bowl of steaming congee
for me and said, "Eat up or you'll be hungry
on your first day of school." He then stood
up and said he had some business to attend
to.

Little did I know that that was the last
time we would see him for a long while.

So many nights I lay awake hoping Ba
would come leaping through the front gates,
but he didn't come until . . .

Ba stirred. His lashes twitched. I didn't know whether I
should stay or go. He must have missed us terribly. I was
Ba's favourite, but Lam was his helper. What could Ba do
without Lam helping him build and fix things?

Days later, three lanky southern soldiers
marched into our house in their uniforms,
guns hanging from their belts. Ba had
been arrested. I cowered behind Ma, who

sat at her sewing machine. Peeking over
her shoulder, I listened as Ma countered
their interrogation with her own questions
regarding Ba's whereabouts. As abruptly as
they emerged, they retreated, leaving me
baffled. Why would they want to know about
Ba's connections or plans? What connections?
What plans? What did it mean, being an
informant for the Viet Cong?

I felt out of sorts standing there in a room so familiar yet
so foreign. The musky smell in the room stirred something
inside me. Ba let out a soft groan as though something was
haunting him in his sleep. He rolled onto his side and I
could see the jagged scar along the edge of his right brow.
The guards at the prison were ruthless, Ma had said. War
is ugly. For two years Ba had been caged and beaten so
he would confess. He was one of the lucky ones though.
While others had been left crippled, Ba had been released
with only a scar and some bruises. But when he returned
home, he didn't come rushing to us as I had envisioned.
He just stood at the front gate until we saw him. I had
already turned eight.

Ba stirred in his sleep. Impulsively, I reached out to
him. Ma had taken us away from him. So far away. He
must have searched far and wide for us.

My hands trembled with excitement as I reached out to him.

As I gently laid my hand on his arm, a frantic sobbing echoed from all directions.

"No, *Ba! Stop, Ba!*"

I jumped back and looked around me, but there was no one else in the room. The cries sounded like they were projecting from me, but they weren't. How could it be? I wasn't crying. I started to shake with fright as the cries kept coming. Where were they coming from?

"No more, *Ba! Please, Ba!*"
I was wailing uncontrollably. I was desperately grabbing hold of Ba's arm, to hold him back, to restrain him, to stop him—
Lam and Muoi were shoved back against the wall. There on the floor was Ma, weeping in pain, holding her large rounded belly.
—to stop him from hurting my mother.

I recoiled and gasped for air.

That smell. That musty smell awakened memories that had laid dormant for so long.

The low afternoon light shone more directly into the middle room. In this light, he looked entirely different from what I remembered. The contours of his face were jagged. His skin was sallow. He had aged and withered.

My heart raced. The room felt smaller and more suffocating. I needed to leave. I stepped back and turned away.

"Who's there?" came a slurred voice behind me.

Maybe he had changed. Maybe he would help. From the looks of things, he didn't have much left either, but still he had a sturdy roof and far more in one room than we had in our whole hut.

"Who are you? What are you doing in here?" he demanded, his voice raspy.

I turned slowly back to face him. He was upright, but using one arm as a crutch, his thinning hair in a sweaty mess. He stared intently at me. Then he furrowed his brow. "Yen?"

"Ba!" I fell to my knees. The sound of my name instantly closed the gap of our years apart. I reached eagerly for his hands, "Yes, it is me, Ba. I am Yen."

He patted my hands, but said nothing.

"Ma and Muoi are planning an escape, Ba." The words poured from my lips before I could catch them. "I don't know what it means, I don't know where, but I'm scared, Ba. I don't want to go—I don't want us to be too far, far from you. Please help Ma. She will stay if you can help her."

Silence.

"What do you think I can do?" His voice was raspy and frigid. His hands slipped away.

I shivered. "Our home in Vinh My village is flooded. We have been struggling to find food, Ba. Ma has been working the land all day and sewing all night. If you could help Ma, maybe with some money, it will help us, to keep us from having to go far away. So, we can remain closer to you."

He said nothing for another minute.

Then he let out a whisper. "Karma."

"What did you say, Ba?" I did not understand. This was not karma. Ma had done nothing wrong to deserve the years of suffering, for us to live so often with famine.

"Where are you going? They're not planning on leaving the country, are they? I wouldn't be surprised if that woman did something so stupid. She'll get you all caught, thrown in prison. You know what they do to people in prison?"

I knew.

"That is why we need your help, Ba."

"Who's this?" said a voice from behind me.

I turned to find the same haughty woman I had encountered at the market. She sashayed into the room from the salon. Her short bob caressed her shiny skin, and her slanted shadowy eyes looked me over from head to toe. Her cream-coloured *áo bà ba* complemented her air of opulence, despite the rusty roof and walls of corrugated metal holding the house together.

The little boy with plump cheeks clung to the tail of her shirt. He gave me a half-smile. I understood now why his eyes looked familiar. The woman propped her hands on her hips and sneered as she approached. "I see your past has come back." She set down her woven handbag and pranced around me. "Looking for money?"

I looked to Ba, but he looked away.

There was nothing more to say. I got back onto my feet and, with my head held high, said, "I don't want anything from either of you." *We will see about karma*, I wanted to say. They deserved each other. I stepped around them and stomped out without looking back.

Then I ran.

As I ran, my eyes watered. And as the tears poured, that child's sobbing echoed in my head. *"No Ba! Stop Ba!"*

I could see the face of that screaming child. She was frightened. Confused.

Faster and faster I ran.

How had I forgotten that child?

I thought I knew Ba. But I never really did.

TEMPLE

I ran as fast and as far as my legs could carry me. Sweat poured from me. The heat and humidity were unbearable. My throat was parched. I was weak and dizzy. By the time I arrived back at the market, I was bent over with exhaustion, my shirt plastered to my back.

My heart thundered in my ears. The Viet Cong had pulled into the city. "Run faster, Muoi!" Ma yelled as she swept me off the ground, only to be thrown down by the force of the first explosion. She threw her body over mine to shield me from the broken debris raining down on us. I shook in her embrace. I was only four then. My ears rang from the blast.

"Run, Lam!" Ma screamed, panicked, as we dove inside another building, breathless,

shaken. Gunfire shattered the air like
firecrackers.

It took another minute before I gathered myself and
realized that there were no firecrackers. All was quiet. The
vendors had cleared out. Even the shrimp lady was gone,
along with Ma's baskets. Only some children in ragged
clothes were loitering about. Bits and pieces of paper and
other garbage littered the grounds.

This was guaranteed punishment, if not banishment
to the eighteenth level of hell for the next thousand years!
At the same time I was rather relieved, not seeing Ma. I
wanted the tears to dry and the dark clouds over my head
to dissipate before she saw me.

While I was deciding where to go from there, two
dusty little boys in tattered clothes and bare feet shuffled
over. Their hair was matted with sweat and dirt. They said
nothing but held out their little palms, their fingernails
caked with dirt. I was flustered. The boys seemed so
desperate. What was the right thing to do? We needed
money as much as they did.

My stomach knotted as I shook my head and stepped
around them, the way others did to Cô Sáu. I hated myself
for it, but at least the money Ma had given me was safely
stashed away.

I meandered haphazardly from shop to shop around

the square in a search of Ma. Some of the shop owners were slouched on red plastic chairs, some with their feet resting on countertops, while others stood around fanning themselves with round bamboo fans. With few shoppers that late in afternoon, all they could do to entertain themselves was stare. I was not at ease. Far too many eyes.

I must have been watching the shopkeepers too, since I did not notice the one-legged man until I bumped into him again, this time knocking him over even more forcefully.

"I'm so, so sorry, mister." I reached down to help him back up and hurriedly gathered his begging can and the few *đồng* scattered over the ground.

He smiled, seeming to recognize me from our previous clumsy encounter. "Not to worry, not to worry, child," he said and hobbled away.

Poor man, I thought. He must have lost his leg in the war or from one of the leftover landmines. Ma said there were mines everywhere across the countryside. Of the people who found them, a fortunate few had only an arm or leg blown off.

I kicked the dirt with my ragged sandals as I wandered slowly through the street. A vendor walked by selling *bánh bao*. For a brief moment I forgot that I was looking for Ma. My mouth salivated for the steamed buns. I reached my hand into my pocket. Maybe I could buy just one.

But there was nothing in my pocket. I checked the other. Nothing. The money was gone! I checked my pockets again. It was really, truly gone!

Where could I have lost it? I panicked. Ma would be livid. I looked down the street from where I had come, but there was nothing on the ground. What could have happened?

I scowled when I realized it. The one-legged man!

Furious, I turned in the direction he had hobbled and saw the tail end of his walking stick disappear into an alley down the road. Ma would be fuming. I had to find that beggar, that thief!

The alley he had disappeared into was long and narrow with overgrown grass. Little light reached down this stretch. I held my breath and flew through the alley, relieved when the sunlight touched my face on the other side.

The beggar was nowhere to be seen. He had vanished into thin air. Instead what I found looked like a jungle of unruly grass and weeds. Toward the centre were rows and rows of tombstones. It was a cemetery.

I remembered that cemetery. A few of the headstones rose from the ground like stone palaces, while many others were smaller, flatter, simpler. Past the far border of the cemetery was the back of a small golden temple with red roofing. The red was faded and chipping while the gold had lost its lustre.

I stepped through the wild grass, careful not to trip and fall, as I made my way to the grave of our ancestors, Bà Ngoại and Ông Ngoại, our maternal grandmother and grandfather. Before we left Ca Mau, Ma had told me her cousin Dì Kim and her husband had promised to look after the headstones for us, but by the looks of the things, they hadn't been doing a very good job. A burning incense had been newly planted in the ground by Ông and Bà Ngoại's greyed rectangular headstones. Ma had been there.

I knelt down and bowed my head to pay my respects. The stones were weathered by the years. I ran my fingers along the faded Chinese inscriptions on Ông Ngoại's stone. My memories too were faded. I could remember though how gentle Ông Ngoại had been. He had migrated from China and worked hard to raise Ma and her two brothers, *Tòa Cũ* and *Soái Cũ*. Ma spoke little Cantonese to us because *he* had only spoken Vietnamese, but Ma explained to us that *Tòa* in Cantonese meant big and *Soái* meant little. *Cũ* was for uncle.

Sadly, the years of working over coal ovens affected Ông Ngoại's breathing until he was unable to breathe anymore. That was long before Tien was born, before Ông Ngoại could see how badly the man who Bà Ngoại told Ma to marry was treating her, before Ông Ngoại could see the hardship we were enduring. Bà Ngoại did not live much longer after Ông Ngoại's passing. She died from a blood infection. If both Ông- Bà Ngoại were alive long enough to see how bad things were, they both would have died from heartache.

At the front of the cemetery, the temple bell chimed. Ma must still be inside.

I had come to this temple with Ma on many occasions to make offerings to Buddha and the deities. We made offerings when we prayed for our uncles' well-being in Saigon during the war. We made offerings when an infection ate at the tip of Muoi's nose. We made offerings when Ma saved Quang from the streets. We even made extra offerings when Tien was born not only safely, despite the trauma Ma had suffered at *his* hands, but in a caul. They said the caul was a sign that Tien was gifted, that she would be protected by *Mụ bà* and the other deities. We first recognized Tien's good fortune when she was only a month old: a bomb had landed just a few feet from where she slept, burrowing into the ground but somehow refusing to detonate.

Smoke from the burning incense inside collected in a thick cloud above the altar. A low hum filled the air as the monks chanted their daily prayers, "*Nam Mô A Di Dà Phật, Nam Mô A Di Dà Phật.*" A soft bell chimed.

Ma was the only one at the altar. She was on her knees with the incense clasped close to her chest. I stood back and watched. Seeing Ma in the soft glow of the candles made my heart ache. Tears welled in my eyes.

I gazed up at the stone Buddha, who sat serenely, cross-legged behind the tiers of burning incense and candles. His hair beaded, eyes closed and lips pursed in a gentle smile. I felt a little resentful. What difference had all our prayers made?

Ma fixed three sticks of incense in the cauldron.

Ma bowed three times and turned to face me as if she knew I'd been standing there. With a quick glare from her, I knew I had to bow to Buddha too. I did so to make her happy.

"Where did you go? I told you not to wander off," Ma said in her usual tone. The baskets were sitting empty on the main steps to the temple. I could not answer. "The shrimp lady said you went to find someone."

I slid my shoulders under the carrying pole. Our hands brushed, and I could feel the roughness of her palm and fingers.

"I went to find an old school friend," I answered, surprised at the smoothness with which the lie rolled off my tongue.

"Oh?" she said.

"Who bought all the crabs and bananas?" I asked, deflecting.

We started to make our way out through the main gate of the temple. "Did you find this friend?"

"I couldn't remember the direction to her house. It's been too long."

"How did you find me then?"

"I knew you would be offering prayers for Ông-Bà Ngoại," I said.

"You remember them?"

"I think of Ông-Bà Ngoại often. I paid my respects to them."

Ma was quiet for a moment. I wasn't sure whether she was about to call me out for telling untruths or praise me for remembering our ancestors.

"The shrimp lady kindly bought all the crab from us, and I was able to sell everything else while you were off. Where is the money I gave you?"

I fell silent again. Before I could think of a plausible excuse, I saw the pitted face of the thieving officer. His eyes glowed red with anger.

"We meet again." He seized my arm and the baskets fell to the ground.

Ma quickly grabbed hold of my other arm and tried to tug me back to her side, but he would not let go.

"What do you want from us?"

"You reported me," he said, uncovering the gun strapped to his belt.

Both Ma and I were stunned. We did not think the official with the square jaw would do anything.

"My back is bleeding from the lashing I received because of you."

"You deserved it!" I said.

But Ma interrupted me. "I am sorry that happened, officer."

"That is all you can say? What are you going to do about it?"

Was he trying to milk more money out of us? He needed another lashing, I thought. I tried wrestling out of his grip as Ma calmly bargained with him. "I did not mean for you to be hurt. We only wanted the officials to know how hard it is for us villagers to make a living."

The officer loosened his grip as if his conscience had awoken, but only for a moment.

"Not so fast." He squeezed my arm so hard I thought it would fall off. "Do you know how I've been humiliated? In front of other officers." There was venom in his eyes.

"You deserved it!" I spat out, more loudly this time.

Out of nowhere, a set of hands pulled me away from him. A little jade pendant dangled from the stranger's neck. Ma hurried to my side. The stranger stood firmly between us and the menacing officer. He did not back down. I held my breath and my hands shook.

To our relief, the officer retreated. Ma quickly dusted me off and checked for injuries.

"Don't be so reckless with your words," she said as

she examined me. "Know when to speak and when to be silent."

I took a deep breath and held my tongue. She would never understand that I could not bear seeing her hurt ever again.

When we turned to thank the stranger with the jade pendant, he was gone.

FABRIC

Dark storm clouds were rolling in. We needed to hurry. Either the clouds or the night would swallow up the sun before we could make it home. Ma towed me to the other side of the city.

"Huong?" said a short balding man when we stepped inside his motor shop. The stunned look on his face was amusing, but I dared not laugh.

Ma greeted him with a nod.

He ushered us to the back of his house, to where the kitchen was. Sitting at the kitchen table, counting their money, was Ma's cousin Dì Kim, dressed in a flowery blue top. Her chin was more pointed than I remembered. When she saw us, Dì Kim turned white as a ghost.

She stumbled onto her feet to welcome us. "It has been too long, Huong. I didn't believe the rumour that you were back in town was true. I didn't think you would ever return." She hid her books and waved her dainty hands, inviting us to sit. "This must be Yen. She is so lovely."

I blushed and sank onto their stubby wooden stool.

She craned her neck and hollered, "Tuyet, pour some tea!" A petite and humble-looking girl rose from where she was squatting outside the kitchen doors. Dì Kim always had hired help, usually high school-aged girls sent up from the poor fishing villages to earn extra money for their family back home. Tuyet scurried into the kitchen like a mouse, made the tea, then scampered back to her little bench on the ground to scrub and hand-wash a pail of clothes at her feet. I sniffed at my top and cringed. It smelled sour. I wondered if anyone else noticed.

"Where are your children?" Ma asked. "They must be all grown up now too."

"Why, yes. Duc is in university. In Saigon. Top of his class. Trung and Huy just received awards too. Everywhere we go, people know these are our boys," she bragged. Then she went on to complain about the business, how poorly they were doing because of the restrictions, but Ma seemed detached. The conversation was forced and uneven, like small talk between strangers, not family. I wondered how she would react if Ma mentioned the height of the weeds around Ông-Bà Ngoại's headstones.

My attention drifted to an army of ants crawling single-file along the edge of the kitchen counter. I could see their destination, a leftover plate of *bánh bèo* and fish sauce. My belly growled, and I rubbed it to silence it.

Ma and Dì Kim lowered their voices to a whisper, which made my ears perk up to listen more intently.

"I am embarrassed to ask for more help," Ma started but then stopped to send me out of the room. I picked myself up and stomped to the front of the shop. *Always too young*, I thought, frowning. I found a bench outside and plopped myself down. The glow of the setting sun behind the rooftop was enveloped by billowing clouds. The wind whistled ever louder. Scattered garbage pirouetted across the ground.

Before long, Ma came marching out.

"Let's go," she said. I was relieved and leapt to my feet, but saw disappointment in her eyes.

Dì Kim and her husband dawdled. "We are sorry again, Huong."

Sorry for what? Ma gave them a half smile to appease their conscience.

"We have a business to run. You understand how hard it is with the war. You saw for yourself how many fewer boats are on the water. Fuel is scarce these days. It is hard for a motor shop like ours to make a living, let alone have any money to lend."

How much money was Ma asking for? What was the cost of the escape Muoi had mentioned? I picked up the baskets and followed Ma.

Citizens were forbidden from hosting anyone in their

homes without first reporting to the officials, Dì Kim said, so they didn't offer us a place to stay for the night. There was no choice but to travel home in the dark.

Ma led us back toward the docks. Though there were only a few dim streetlights, I didn't need them to see that Ma was trying to conceal her tears. I could forgive Dì Kim for not being able to care for Ông-Bà Ngoại's grave, but I couldn't forgive her for turning her back on us when Ma needed her help. If our own relatives weren't willing to help us, who would?

"What if those officials are at the dock?" I asked.

Ma kept walking. Large drops of rain started falling on our heads, and we picked up our pace.

"Who do you suppose that man was?" I asked.

"What man?"

"The man with the jade pendant. The one who helped chase the thieving officer away. Do you know him?"

Ma stopped, looked at the two paths that lay before us and took us down an abandoned road.

"We have one more stop."

Before long, we stood in front of another house, its rusty metal gate pulled almost to a close. It was just ajar enough for my head to squeeze through. I recognized it. It was the fabric store that Ma and I used to frequent. I could see that the walls, once lined with rolls and rolls of fabric coils in every colour, texture and pattern, were now virtually barren. No silk or satin. Only brown, white or black polyester and cotton.

"Thanh?" Ma called softly.

We waited. Soon a short lady with a black mole just above the left corner of her lip came shuffling out to announce, "We're closing, dear customers."

"Thanh, it's me. Huong."

"Huong?" she came closer and her face lit up. She quickly opened the gate. "Come in, come in out of the rain." Cô Thanh stuck her head back out, checking to see that no one was watching us, then pulled the gates completely shut. The rain poured like rocks from the sky.

"It's so late. Where are you headed? You have to stay the night."

"We wouldn't want to impose," Ma said. The fluorescent light bulbs flickered above our heads. A pair of dark geckos dashed across the ceiling.

"What imposition? There's no imposition between old friends. Please come in, come in." She led us to the sitting area in the midsection of her house.

"But don't you have to report to the officials?"

"You still worry too much, Huong. They've already become rich off of us."

Ma used to bring me to Cô Thanh's store when she offered sewing lessons to young students in the neighbourhood. To Ma's dismay, I was never patient enough to sit and learn the trade, but it was consolation enough knowing that Muoi had inherited her love of sewing.

A stooped elderly woman stepped into the room while Cô Thanh went into the kitchen to fetch some snacks. Ma and I stood up to bow politely, but the elderly woman's eyes were too clouded by the white curtain of cataracts to see us clearly. It was Cô Thanh's mother. She had aged and shrunken since we had last seen her. She smiled and carefully felt her way along the furniture. Ma met her halfway to help her into a seat next to us.

The dim light from the hanging lamp flickered; the wobbly ceiling fan clicked on and off. When Cô Thanh reminded her mother who we were, the mother's smile widened. Cô Thanh laid out a plate of sliced ambarella and mangoes and glasses of iced water. The fruits were marinated in a sauce of salt and sugar to enhance the sour flavour. "*Cốc chua* and *xoài chua*," she offered, and my taste buds shrieked with delight. She had not changed at all. I remembered how she had snuck little candy treats into my palms whenever Ma came to purchase her needles and thread.

"A slice for you, child," Cô Thanh's mother said, placing a piece of mango between my fingers. "And another," she said as soon as I had finished the first juicy piece. She must have heard my stomach growling from across the room. When the elderly mother leaned over a third time to set down her glass of water, I saw a jade pendant around her neck, like that stranger at the temple.

When Ma asked about the whereabouts of Cô Thanh's husband, Cô Thanh shook her head and whispered, "They've taken him to a labour camp. To re-educate him, they say. It's been three years."

"They are terrible," her mother grieved. "We can only pray that they return him to us one day soon."

Ma shook her head.

"Do not worry about us, Huong. He will come home. And we are managing. One thing the war has taught us is to live within our means. We are prepared for times like these."

"And your son?"

Cô Thanh diverted her eyes for a moment. She knew the walls had ears. Luckily the rain muffled our voices.

Cô Thanh's mother answered loudly, "He is dead." She pointed to the altar where a faded black and white photograph of Cô Thanh's son hung. I could barely make out the face in the photograph. An incense was burning for him.

"I am so sorry," Ma said. "I thought I . . ." Her voice trailed off, but she must have been thinking what I was thinking. The stranger who helped us looked an awful lot like Cô Thanh in profile.

"There is no future for our children here. They barely laid down their arms, and now they're drafting more young boys to die for them, fighting in Cambodia." She glanced around and whispered, "We cannot lose our only son."

I was confused. Was he dead or alive?

Cô Thanh's voice trembled. "If he stays, we will lose him. If he goes, we will lose him. At least there is hope for him if he goes." I was lost, but Ma seemed to understand what Cô Thanh was trying to say. There was a lightning crash and the lights flickered again.

"How can any of us *người hoa* keep living like this, barely surviving?" Cô Thanh whispered.

"You are brave, Huong," Cô Thanh continued. "Some of us have little choice but to stay. There's still so much that ties us to our country." She looked at her elderly mother. I could sense Cô Thanh's grief. After another moment of reflection, Cô Thanh turned to me and smiled. "Yen, during the height of the war, when it was difficult to find even a grain of rice, your mother shared hers. No others would."

The gate rattled with the peal of lightning. Then everything went dark.

YAMS

I felt like I had only just closed my eyes when Ma tapped me on the shoulder to get me up and moving again. The roosters crowed, the street vendors chanted.

Ma and Cô Thanh had talked into the early hours. It had been impossible to sleep. Cô Thanh made sure our baskets were weighted down with yams, a bag of rice, extra spools of thread and a few metres of fabric. She had insisted that we take some rice. Between her and her mother, she said, they could spare some. As we bid farewell, Ma and Cô Thanh broke down in tears. I knew that this was it. We would never see them again.

On our way to the docks, we passed a warehouse where a crowd of people had gathered for their ration of rice. The sun had barely cracked open the morning and people were already waiting in line.

"How can this last our family for the month?" a man asked, holding out the small sack of rice he was given.

"That's how much you get. I don't care if it lasts or

not," an official replied, his tone colder than ice.

"Take pity on our hungry children," pleaded a woman in the crowd, but I could see that the officials were unmoved.

Ma urged me to hasten my steps. We couldn't risk being stopped and searched.

While people poured in to the morning markets, we threaded against the crowd and found a boat willing to take us upriver to where our rowboat was parked. As we were about to climb in, a gruff voice startled us from behind. "Not so fast."

It was him, the pitted-face officer who attacked us by the temple. Ma lowered the baskets to the ground. Ma nudged me to step behind her, but I refused to move.

"What do you have in your baskets?" he asked, with one eye on me and the other on the baskets.

"Food from the market," I said rather politely, before Ma had a chance to find her words. I said what I was sure she would have said. "You are welcome to inspect." Ma's eyes widened. I don't know whether she was surprised at my diplomacy or disapproving of my tactics. It was a gamble that could cost us everything.

He said nothing at first, as if he too was puzzled. He hesitated for another second, then lifted the fabric that covered one of the baskets. I dared not even breathe a sigh of relief when he saw only yams underneath.

"Your mother must have given you a good whipping to put you back in your place," he said, and marched off.

I was dumbfounded, but we didn't dare delay our departure. As our boat pushed away from the dock, a sadness came over me. The hustle and bustle of Ca Mau, on land and in the water, faded as the distance grew between us and the town. I glanced over to Ma, but she showed no emotion. As the aromas dissipated, the noise muted and the last glimpse of the city passed, my grief turned to emptiness.

I didn't know what to expect when we got back to the village. I shouldn't have been surprised to find the floodwater still high.

"Ma's home! Ma's home!" Tien exclaimed when she saw us approaching. She and Quang were paddling around outside with Lam. Ma smiled at them as we steered into the house. Lam pulled his boat beside us and helped Ma lift the baskets onto the loft.

It was hard looking at Lam in the eye knowing how he used to take pride in building and fixing things alongside *him*. If Lam was at all curious about *his* whereabouts or wellbeing, he did not let on. I couldn't bear telling Lam the truth about how little *he* really cared about us, how *he* was no better a person.

Muoi stood up from behind the sewing machine and

dragged the baskets in. Ma was pleased that Muoi had found neighbours who needed new outfits made. I held up the fabric Cô Thanh had given us and smiled at the possibility of a new shirt and trousers. Muoi looked at me and grimaced, as if she knew that I had found Ba. I looked away.

Tien grabbed two yams from the baskets and waved them around. She fluttered like butterflies do, and we all laughed. If I had been a little younger, I would have danced too, to celebrate the moment. But of course Ma said, "There's work to be done," and the next minute I was heading out with Lam and Quang to chop some more wood. I didn't even get a chance to look inside the other basket.

Bác Minh joined us for dinner at Ma's request. We were lucky to have found him floating in his boat along the river. According to Lam, Bác Minh had been away too. I was certain he was out looking for Trinh's siblings. Over a few short days, the lines and crevices on Bác Minh's face had deepened, his shoulders slumped more. Bác Minh had aged twenty years in the span of a couple days. His eyes, if I stared into them long enough, were a mirror that reflected horrors and sorrows, of which he neither would nor could speak.

Bác Minh asked about Ca Mau when we were gathered

in a circle around the pot of rice and yams.

"Viet Cong everywhere," Ma said as she scrubbed the dirt off Tien's hands and face. No matter how caked in dirt and mud things were around us, Ma made sure we were clean.

"They are ruthless!" I said. I did not hold back my contempt for them. "That pitted-face officer is a thieving wretched communist," I said, imitating what I had heard some adults say.

Bác Minh shook his head disapprovingly. "Hatred in the heart is as heavy as stones in your soul. The weight will sink you, child. War brings out the worst in people. I have seen far more ugliness in a few years than I would want to see in a few lifetimes." He looked away.

"They sure hate us though," I said. "I don't understand why they don't like *người hoa*. We're Vietnamese too."

"Lam and Muoi will be going back to Saigon in a day or two, depending on the weather," Ma said.

"So soon," Bác Minh said softly. His tone betrayed no sense of surprise or grief. He asked no questions, as if he already knew.

Lam added, "Bác Minh, you are welcome to use some of the wood we chopped today. And there is a barrel of fresh tide water that I fetched yesterday." Bác Minh smiled and nodded his thanks. It would be easier to use our fresh water than having to boil the stagnant floodwater around his house every time he had to drink.

Seeing Quang and Tien waiting politely for their food made me even more restless. "Why must Muoi and Lam go first? Can't we go together?" I knew why Lam and Muoi were leaving for Saigon by themselves. Ma didn't want to stir suspicion with us leaving all at once.

Muoi said, "We have to go back to school."

Why won't they tell me anything?

"Then when will we see you again?"

"You ask too many questions, child," Ma answered.

"I'm not a child! I know we're preparing to escape!" I used the word not knowing what it meant.

"Hush!" Ma snapped. Quang and Tien hung their heads, confused by my behaviour in front of Bác Minh. Muoi shot me a stern look. Ma took in a deep breath and turned to Bác Minh. "You must be tired." She passed him a pair of chopsticks and a bowl of rice sprinkled with a pinch of sea salt.

"One cannot rest when the spirits are still restless," Bác Minh said.

"*Nam Mô A Di Dà Phật*," Ma said.

"Nothing worse for the heart than when parents live past the days of their children."

I didn't know if Bác Minh meant Trinh and his parents, but Trinh's parents had not been seen since the storm. I felt Bác Minh's sorrow. I often wondered about Bác Minh's family, whether he had children, how many and where they were. I never had enough courage to ask, since he was so reluctant to speak about his life. But the loss of Trinh and his siblings had stirred something inside him.

Ma invited us to start eating. Tien groaned as soon as Ma broke open one of the yams.

I broke mine in two as well. As the steam rose from its dark flesh, I saw the cause of Tien's reaction. White worms threaded the inside. My stomach churned.

Ma took each of the yams from us, picked out the worms, then placed them back in our hands.

I was hungry. Nothing could go to waste.

The next day, before she and Lam set out for Saigon, Muoi pinned me to the corner of the loft and asked if I had seen *him*. I was taken aback. Why did it matter? The thought of *him* made my blood boil again. *He* could die for all I cared.

"I met no one we knew," I said. And that was the end of that.

THREADS

A storm was coming. I dug my feet into the muddy ground. As hard as Ma tried to drag me out to sea with her, I would not budge.

"No, Ma," I cried, "don't make me go!" Waves roared furiously onto shore. Swept out to sea, Trinh and his siblings thrashed about. Then a multitude of faces cried out, as they had so many times before. One of those faces was Ba's, and an anger grew within me as I sank deeper and deeper.

I woke with a start. My temples throbbed. The same dream again, each time more troubling than the last. Bác Minh once told me that dreams are windows into our future. This was a warning. I was sure of it, and it ate at me.

Something whimpered. I looked around. It was Quang. I rolled back onto my side and watched a tiny red ant crawl hastily into a crooked crack at the far end of the floor.

The floodwaters had receded. We could finally shuffle with ease through the ankle-deep water.

Between Ma and I, we were able to sell off most of our belongings, but we kept Ma's sewing machine. We still needed it. To those who bought our tools and household items, Ma would only say that we were moving to Saigon. I had no idea what was in store for us. The bombs and soldiers, the ragged clothes, the muddy fields and dusty roads, they were all I knew.

"Quang's crying, Yen!" Ma called up from below. "Why aren't you checking on him?"

I grumbled, rolled back over and slithered closer to him. He was always trouble. When I had a closer look at him, I regretted my delay. His cheeks were flushed, his breathing shallow and rapid. Beads of sweat collected at his hairline. His vacant gaze met my own.

"Are you alright?"

He groaned.

"Ma! He's sick!" His forehead was on fire.

Ma came up to the loft with a coin-sized tub of Tiger balm. She quickly lathered him with the ointment, across the forehead, around his neck, over his tummy, back and feet. As she smeared, she murmured under her breath, "*Nam Mô A Di Dà Phật, Nam Mô A Di Dà Phật.*"

"Is he going to be alright?" I asked.

Ma would not say.

I slipped downstairs and boiled a pot of rice congee. Congee always made us feel better when we were sick. It scared me how frail Quang looked.

"Go downriver for me," Ma said as she spoon-fed him the congee. There were a few tailored outfits she needed to deliver.

I lured Tien with a banana and took her with me. As we passed the stilt house in the folds of the palm trees at the bend in the river, I could see the thin young mother with her growing belly watching her daughter bathe on the shallow banks of the river. Her little son sat on her lap. Standing on their metal roof, a man spread out his fishing net to dry. It must have been her husband. I hoped he was having better luck than Cô Lien's husband.

The little girl wasn't so cantankerous anymore. She giggled and waved to me from the water, and I smiled and waved back. Tien wanted to join in on the fun in the water, but I reminded her that we had chores to do. I briefly made eye contact with the young mother and smiled. It was a sad smile though, as I knew that we would be gone long before her new baby arrived.

The trees grew denser beyond the river bend. The monkeys were out in abundance, climbing and dangling from the trees. Tien giggled and pointed at them, so I pulled in closer for her to watch. One of the little monkeys scurried down and snatched the banana from her hand. Tien shrieked and the little monkey darted back up to the high branches. I could hardly contain my laughter, but kept it down enough to console her, like a good big sister.

The customer we were making the delivery to lived in a two-storey yellow tube house that loomed over the many dilapidated homes flanking their land.

A lady with tight curls met us at the door. She seemed out of place, dressed in a silky floral *áo bà ba*, when so few flowers bloomed around us. Not many could afford to curl their hair and dress like her. She had an air to her. Perhaps she had done something good in her past life to deserve all that.

I handed over the three traditional *áo dài* dresses Ma had painstakingly sewn. The lady grabbed them from me and disappeared into the house. Tien and I waited patiently at the shiny ceramic entrance. The ceramic was so white I was sure we could have eaten right off the floor. Ants couldn't penetrate that floor or those walls.

Tien started to dance around. "I need to pee."

"Can you hold it?" I said.

The lady was taking her time checking the outfits.

"I can't," Tien said, dancing more vigorously.

The lady returned with a look of displeasure on her face. She had a much bigger bag in her hand.

"Take this back to your mother. The collar is too tight

and the sleeves are too long."

"But Ma never makes a mistake in her measurements." Ma was known as the best seamstress in town.

"Do you doubt me?"

I bit my tongue to answer politely, as Ma would have expected. "No."

"I'm doing your mother a favour. While she's at it, there are two other outfits I'd like her to alter. I need them back by tomorrow."

"What about the payment, *Cô*?" I wanted to throw up, being so polite.

"I'll pay you when your mother has done what I've asked. Is your mother teaching you to take advantage of our generosity?"

I felt an intense heat on my face. Ma had worked night and day on those outfits. It took all my willpower to resist dumping the whole bag of clothes overboard. But as we rowed away, I noticed a puddle on the floor where Tien had stood, and I smirked.

Bác Minh was outside mending the side wall of his house when we passed. He waved to us and walked over to the edge of the river to greet us.

"Why does the colour of your face match the grey sky?"

I shrugged. Tien took it upon herself to answer for me. "Quang's sick."

Bác Minh frowned, but he waited to hear more. I told him how Quang looked that morning. Bác Minh said nothing but looked concerned.

"We met a mean lady," Tien blurted. I sighed and told Bác Minh about the unpleasant encounter with the unreasonable customer.

Bác Minh nodded gently. "I see." Then he said, "Why should your day be grey when she has no power over the sun? I see the sun is still shining. Rich people easily lose perspective, my child. You should not." He smiled and asked us to wait. He waded into his house and came back out with a sack of fruit peels. "Give this to your Ma. She'll know what to do."

I thanked him, but I wasn't ready to leave.

"How can you sleep with so much on your mind, child?" Bác Minh asked.

"I still see Trinh in my dreams. I cannot sleep."

Bác Minh nodded as if he already knew. "In time, sleep will come. Trinh is at rest now."

"But how?"

"When a child sings his songs, a mother's heart will follow. Back in the womb of the mother, he lies. His spirit is at peace."

"You mean . . . the brown cocoons?" I mumbled.

"A new life is formed."

I shuddered, picturing the sacks we had passed on our

journey weeks earlier. The higher grounds had risen above the water, so the bodies must have been buried.

"But the dreams—"

"Answers to your fears lie in your dreams," he said, and left it at that.

Ma was disappointed hearing of the customer's demands, but as usual she said little. She put me straight to work snipping the threads at the seams. Meanwhile, she threw the fruit peels into a pot of boiling water. When the brew was fully steeped, Ma set the steaming pot of peels down in the middle of the loft and held Quang's head, covered with a towel, over the steam. His lips were dry and cracked, his eyes bloodshot.

After the steaming, Quang's breathing eased, but he was far from looking better. I fed him more congee. By that evening, Quang's persistent fever gave Ma cause to coin him. She lifted his shirt, revealing his protruding rib cage and spine.

With the edge of the Tiger balm lid, Ma scraped the sides of his neck and down along his spine until purplish beads appeared on the surface of his skin.

"That is the poisonous air," Ma said.

After much screaming and squirming, Quang fell asleep, exhausted by the painful treatment.

Ma said coining was just as good as seeing a doctor. She

had cured many of our illnesses without having to make the long, arduous trip downriver. We couldn't afford one anyway.

Ma spent the rest of the evening huddled over the sewing machine, her foot on the pedal, making it sing. Back and forth she swayed as the dress flowed between the wheel and spools of thread. The sounds of the sewing machine were usually a comforting song to my ears, but that night it cried more than it sang. Ma had once said, "People will step on you when you are poor and have little education." Her customer had been doing just that.

When it got too dark to thread the needles, Ma worked by the light of the kerosene lamp to get the work done.

A sudden clatter outside startled us. Bác Minh appeared at our doorway, breathless and anxious. I had never seen him in such a panicked state.

"You must leave now!" he shouted.

STILTS

"There are eyes everywhere," Bác Minh panted. "There's been talk. They know you're leaving. Men are coming for you."

I put down the scissors. Sweat was pouring down Bác Minh's shiny forehead.

Ma met him halfway down the ladder. "Are you sure?"

"Words have fallen on the wrong ears. Men will try to rob you tonight. They think there will be money here."

Ma shook her head in disbelief. "We have nothing here. Only the children . . ."

Who could have told them about our plans? Was it the people at the market square? Was it Ma's cousin, or the people who came here to purchase our things?

"Muoi and Lam," I said, pulling Tien and Quang closer to me. Ma had sent what Cô Thanh had given us with Muoi and Lam.

"They will be safe," Ma said.

I wasn't convinced. We had not heard from them since

they had left for Saigon. There was no way of knowing if they made it there safely. The only thing we knew was that we were to meet at Tòa Cū's house on the next full moon.

Something rustled in the leaves. I jumped. We waited. When nothing happened, Ma said, "Gather your things!" Ma had already packed a cloth handbag with a few essentials—an extra set of clothes for each of us, some food to snack on, a tub of Tiger balm and her sewing kit. Years of war had prepared her to run at a moment's notice.

I rushed the kids down the ladder. When I came back to grab my notebook, the clothes Ma had been working on for the curly-haired lady slipped from the sewing machine to the ground, the silk material strewn across the dusty floor. I barely noticed when I walked over them.

Ma carried Quang into the boat while Tien toddled along.

"Come with us, Bác Minh," I said, expecting him to climb on after us.

But he didn't move. Bác Minh wrinkled his eyes, shook his head and chuckled. "My legs are too crooked and feeble, my child."

"We will help you, Bác Minh. I can take care of you." I tugged at his hand, but he pulled back.

"Silly child, this is the land of my ancestors. All that I have is here. My children and grandchildren have waited a long time for me. This is where I belong. This is my future. Your future is out there." It was the first time he spoke of his family. I refused to listen, and he refused to move. He nudged me forward. "Go, my child." Then he turned to Ma. "I will wait for them," he said. "I can delay them."

Ma ushered me onto the boat. She stood by Bác Minh's side for a moment longer. "Until we meet again."

He smiled and pushed our boat into the river. The flickering of the lamp in the loft lit up the sewing machine that had kept us alive all those years. As we drifted away, I watched Bác Minh standing all alone, his frail lonesome silhouette hunched over.

There were no stars in the sky. The moon was nowhere to be seen. My stomach was in knots, not knowing what to expect. As we approached the stilt house at the bend, beams of flashlights flickered through the dense trees. My gut twisted. I stood up and took hold of the oars in Ma's hands. "Quick, turn toward that house."

For once, Ma did not question me. She steered the boat up to the stilt house and gently rapped on the door. The flashlights were coming closer. It felt like forever before the young mother swung open the door. As soon as she saw our faces, she ushered us beneath the house.

There was just enough room between the water and the house for our boat to fit. "Lie down!" Ma said. With one swift stroke of the oar, she slipped us to the farthest corner of the space. I could hear Ma's pounding heart. Tien and Quang didn't make a sound.

The little boy above started to cry, as if he knew something sinister was at hand. The wooden floor creaked as the mother paced, humming to her child. "Daddy will be home in the morning. The midwife's coming soon. You'll be a big brother soon, so be my good little boy."

Then came a loud knock. All went still up above. I covered Tien's mouth and we held our breaths. The weighted steps of the young mother crossed to the door.

"Who is it at this late hour?" she asked.

No answer.

The creak of the door opening.

"What can I do for you?"

"Are you Tran Tu Huong?" said a gruff voice.

"No, I am not." The young mother's voice was shaky.

"A woman with older children. A house with a sewing machine."

"I do not know her. You must be mistaken."

They pulled away, their flashlight pointed upstream.

Ma waited until the rippling of their oars had disappeared before pulling us out from hiding. She thanked the young mother.

"Do not thank me, Huong. It is the least I could do. Your daughter gave us rice when my children were starving."

Ma glanced at me, puzzled. But she said nothing and propelled us quickly around the bend.

We hadn't travelled far when the stillness of the night suddenly exploded. The sound of a gunshot reverberated through the consuming darkness, echoing over the water from far behind us. Monkeys shook the trees, shrieking.

Ma stopped, and the children clung to each other.

I looked back.

Then all fell silent, except for Bác Minh's voice, echoing in my head.

My heart felt like it too had exploded into a million pieces. Tears rolled down my cheeks.

COCONUTS

One stretch of river was so humid it was suffocating. Through the oppressive air came whispers and whimpering, I could not tell from where. Without moonlight, I could not make out any other boats or houses. My hair stood on end. Ma would not say what the noises were, but she knew.

Bác Minh had told stories about parts of the river still haunted by civilians and soldiers killed during the war. A terrible stench rose out of the stale water. Ma paddled faster. The voices were unsettling for her too.

I bolted up, grasping to hold on to something, anything to steady my dizzy head. Nauseated, I scrambled onto my side to throw up, but there was nothing in my stomach to bring up. Bac Minh's face appeared then disappeared into the darkness that blanketed us. Pain gnawed at my stomach.

Unsure which way was up or down, left or right, I stood up to regain my bearings. The ground gave way, swaying

116

back and forth with little splashes and splatters. We were still afloat.

"Sit down, Yen!" Ma said. "You'll flip the boat before we get to shore."

I lowered myself onto the seat and realized the two children were curled into little balls at my feet. The boat slowed and tapped gently against the dock. We had arrived. Ma grabbed the ledge to pull us in. Her silhouette seeming both fragile and strong at the same time as she had paddled long and hard all night.

As Ma finished tying up the boat, a rooster welcomed the morning. The darkness soon dissipated.

"Where are we?" I asked.

"Bac Lieu. We'll catch the bus to Saigon from here."

The rays of morning sun sparkled through the slits between rows and rows of tilted slumping buildings. Ma woke Quang to get him on his feet. I lifted Tien up and out of the boat and carried her on my hip. Tien weighed on me, and my worn-out slippers provided little protection against the jagged rocks and pebbles paving our way. But Quang moved slowly, so I did not lag too far behind.

After a few false turns, we finally reached the bus terminal. It was in a simple square. Along one side were wooden stalls where early-morning vendors congregated. Three buses sat in the middle. A crowd of passengers was lined up for the bus to Ho Chi Minh City, the new name for Saigon.

"Wait here," Ma said, and walked over to the ticket kiosk. Quang squatted on the ground, while Tien clung to my neck. There were so many people looking to travel to Saigon. *I hope there is room for us on the bus*, I thought.

"Boarding for Ho Chi Minh!" the attendant announced. The engines revved and the passengers filed onto the bus. I stretched my neck, anxiously looking for Ma to see if she found tickets for us. Tien stirred in my arms, rubbed her eyes, then whimpered, "Thirsty."

Ma was busy sorting out the fares. I looked around to see what our options were for a drink. I shuffled along the stalls. There were chopped sugar canes and sugar cane juice sold in little plastic bags, durian cakes and sesame crackers, but I did not have any change on me. Ma needed all our money for the bus.

"Thirsty," Tien said again. Quang limped along beside us but made no requests.

"Not now," I said.

A short elderly woman came hopping toward us. On her shoulders were baskets filled with coconuts that looked heavier than she did. I recognized the crooked smile. It was the coconut lady Ma and I had encountered on the river.

"Fresh coconut. Fresh coconut for sale!" She chanted

her song as she had on the river and, in a blink, pirouetted around us dropping a cut coconut into my hands.

"Sorry, I don't have any money, *Bác*." I tried to hand the coconut back.

She smiled at me and said, "Coconut milk is good for the ill and the temperamental. Gives you energy for long travels." She continued on her way without another word. I didn't know what to say. How did she know Quang was ill? When I realized she wasn't returning for payment, I handed the coconut to Tien. She guzzled it down voraciously. That coconut was like an endless fountain, and more milk poured out for me and Quang.

Ma returned looking dejected and upset. "They have no more tickets. The scalper is asking for an outrageous amount."

"Last call for boarding! Ho Chi Minh!"

The attendant rounded up the last few passengers. Desperate, Ma turned to the remaining travellers to ask if anyone could spare tickets.

My stomach sank as the bus door folded shut. I grabbed Ma's hands and we cut through the crowd to the door of the bus. I rapped on it. "Please, driver!"

The door opened and the driver called out Ma's name. I could not believe my eyes. It was Cô Lien's husband, the fisherman. We hadn't seen them for weeks. He gestured for us to climb on.

"Lien just had surgery. I have to work extra to pay off the medical bills."

"I'm so sorry," Ma said.

He shook his head. "If it weren't for your help, Huong, we wouldn't have had this second chance. A grain of rice means everything." He asked us to sit.

We wormed our way through the pack of gloomy-looking passengers and squeezed in at the back seat. As soon as we sat down, Ma succumbed to her exhaustion and fell asleep. Tien was squished in my arms, while Quang was sandwiched between Ma and I.

As we sat waiting for the bus to depart, I gazed out at the solemn faces of the people waiting for the other buses. It was such a relief to be on the bus, but a sickening feeling grew in the pit of my stomach. I wasn't sure if it was for what we had already lost or from fear of what we might be about to lose.

SAiGON

We were exhausted. It took an entire day to travel from Bac Lieu to Saigon by bus. The longest waits were at the ferry crossings at Bac My Thuan and Bac Can Tho, hours at each one. Saigon used to be loud, congested and beautifully chaotic, Ma said. Now, speakers fixed at street corners blared the songs of the new army, loud enough to drown out the heavy rain.

The rusty metal gate screeched open. Soái Cú, Ma's younger brother, was surprised to see us standing in the dark alley outside their house. We were thoroughly drenched.

"Come in, come in, it's approaching curfew." He swept us inside, "You were supposed to arrive when the moon was full."

"We had to leave quickly," Ma said. "Men were searching for us. What curfew?"

"People are prohibited on the streets late at night," he said, closing the gate behind us. Then he announced, "Siu

121

Heung and the kids are here!" Siu Heung was Cantonese for little fragrant flower. No one called Ma that in Ca Mau. "Soái Kiểm! Siu Heung and the children are here. They are hungry and exhausted! Bring them towels to dry off."

I only had vague memories of their home. We had visited once or twice before. It was very long from front to back and very tall, rising three levels.

Soái Cũ's wife, Soái Kiểm, came rushing out to meet us. "*Neih hou ma?*" she asked as she draped a towel around each of us. I knew just enough Cantonese from listening to Ma to understand the basic greetings. *All is good*, I wanted to say, *now that we're here*, but I didn't know the words. Soái Kiểm took Tien from Ma's arms to cuddle. "It's been too long, Siu Heung," Soái Kiểm said as she pinched Tien's cheeks. "Such beautiful children."

A boy and a girl, both a little younger than myself and looking like they had been pulled from their sleep, also came out to greet us. They smiled warmly but Tien and Quang refused to crack a smile back, too tired to be polite. They introduced themselves as Hieu and Anh. Hieu was a year younger but was already taller than me. Anh had a short hair cut like her older brother. Soái Kiểm handed me a dry shirt to change into. I nodded my thanks.

"Pity the children. Such a long journey for them. We need to get them out of these wet clothes before they get sick."

Ma and Soái Cú exchanged a few more words in Cantonese as he led us to the back of the house. The dim fluorescent bulbs flickered with each lightning crash, and the tin roof drummed under the pelting rain. Their house had tiled floor and grey walls that separated their front foyer from the middle sitting room and the back kitchen area. We walked past an altar with black-and-white framed photographs of Ông Ngoại and Bà Ngoại. A stick of incense burned for them. A plate of fruits had been set in front of the pictures as offerings. Placards with columns of Chinese symbols hung on either side.

The photographs intrigued me. We hadn't seen many photographs, especially of the family. Ông Ngoại's eyes were mesmerizing. Looking into them I was transported to a different place and time, when Ông Ngoại first immigrated from China. *It must have been a lot of work to build a life in a new country*, I thought. Hopefully, the prayers offered here would help our ancestors lie in peace despite the neglect their headstones had endured in Ca Mau.

Soái Kiểm sat us around the kitchen table and Soái Cú offered us a glass of water. "You arrived on a good day, Siu Heung. There's electricity today."

Ma wasn't impressed. "Are Muoi and Lam asleep?" Ma asked instead.

The mood dampened. Soái Cú closed his eyes and

bowed his head. Soái Kiểm pursed her lips.

"Muoi and Lam are not here, Siu Heung," Soái Cũ said. "They're alright though."

Ma's shoulders relaxed, and she sat back on the chair.

"I've telephoned Tòa Cũ," Soái Cũ continued. "He's on his way here. He can explain the situation better than we can."

It was Tòa Cũ who had purchased the boat that Ma said would take us to freedom. I marvelled at Soái Cũ's little black rotary phone. I had never met anyone with a telephone. Soái Kiểm was a doctor so I could see why she needed a phone.

Soái Kiểm brought us bowls of rice and and salted dried fish. The kids and I chomped on the rice as if we hadn't been fed in years.

"You are really hungry!" Soái Cũ said.

But Ma hardly touched her food. She did not ask anymore about Lam and Muoi until Tòa Cũ arrived.

Ma's face lit up when Tòa Cũ came in. He was tall, dignified and scholarly and had soft eyes like Ông Ngoại. Ma had not seen both brothers at the same time in years, but they strung together their Cantonese words fluidly as if they had never been apart.

Soon Ma placed the chopsticks across her rice bowl. "Tien and Quang, go upstairs with your cousins."

I didn't move.

Ma turned to me. "You can stay."

All at once, I felt older.

"Muoi and Lam have already gone," Tòa Cũ said softly, almost in a whisper.

"Left? By themselves?" Ma asked angrily. A chill came over me and I shivered. Muoi and Lam had the gold taels we had hidden in Cô Thanh's rice bag, which would pay for our family's place on the boat.

"Three days ago. They are with trusted friends."

"But they can't go without us!" I exclaimed. I felt a pang in my heart. Was this what my dreams were warning me about? The brothers and sisters lost at sea? How would we ever find them?

"We had no choice, Siu Heung," said Tòa Cũ. "Our boat had no room left. A friend was willing to take them on his boat."

Ma's eyes grew damp, but she said nothing. Her eyes settled over me.

"I had to make a decision, Siu Heung."

"Where was their boat going?" Ma asked.

Soái Cũ said, "Malaysia."

"Why Malaysia? Is it safe there?"

"Yes, I hope so. From there they can go to America, or Australia. Anywhere."

"They had all of our gold taels," Ma said. There was silence, and Ma knew—I knew—that there was not enough money to pay for the rest of us. It would be eight gold taels per head to get on the boat.

"But Muoi and Lam . . . we have to find them," I insisted.

The rain poured outside, but the silence inside was deafening.

"How can I live without my children?" Ma asked Tòa Cũ. "They are my life. I have to follow them."

"There's no more room in our boat. That's why we had to send Muoi and Lam with our friend."

Ma began to cry. I had never seen her cry before.

Soái Cũ looked to Soái Kiểm, who gave him a nod. Soái Cũ said, "Siu Heung, your family can take our place. Your family needs to be together. We don't know anyone out there. Our family is here, and we have a life here. What are we going to do overseas, anyway? We've already paid the bribe, so you won't be stopped."

"But if you stay, you could be arrested," Ma said. "You could be rounded up and sent to a labour camp."

"Don't worry about us. Kiểm is a doctor. They need doctors here. They won't bother us."

I felt a heaviness on my shoulders. What should we do? Perhaps the answer did lie in our dreams, as Bác Minh had said—and my dreams were of the sea.

"What do you say, Siu Heung?" Tòa Cũ said. "Will you go with us?"

Ma's eyes drifted into the distance. "We have come this

far. There's nothing left here for us. There is no future for my children here. Our lives are in God's hands."

SONGS

We had one day left in Saigon. I sat at the kitchen table with Ma and Soái Cũ. We had just woken from an afternoon nap. Tien played quietly upstairs with Hieu and Anh, while Quang continued to catch up on his sleep. Soái Kiếm had told us to get extra rest so we would have enough energy for the long journey. I hadn't slept all night. I was worried sick about getting on the boat, about never seeing Muoi and Lam again. Outside, the constant loop of songs grated on my nerves, so much so that the words were echoing in my head.

"This song is about a young girl going up the mountain to set sharp bamboo traps that will kill tigers and panthers," Soái Cũ told me.

"Why would they play that over and over again?"

"If you hear it enough times, child, you might want to be a fighter."

I shuddered.

"The tigers and panthers are the American invaders,"

Soái Kiểm said when she stepped into the kitchen, setting down a couple of green papayas her patients had given her as payment for medical care. "Don't speak so loudly when my patients are here," she gently scolded Soái Cũ. "It's a good thing the chatty old lady I just examined is already going deaf."

Soái Cũ shrugged and carried on. "The songs are a form of re-education, Yen. They remind us that someone's always watching. Everyone is afraid."

"Hush," Soái Kiểm said. "The walls have ears."

"The Viet Cong even burned many of our books, including some rare and precious ones. They want to get rid of everything that might remind people of the past."

"Not all books were burned," Soái Kiểm whispered. She lifted open the base of a small cupboard, revealing a small stack of books hidden underneath the shelving. "I didn't go to school all those years to let them destroy everything."

I smiled at her defiance.

"There has been so much upheaval," she said, wiping tears from her eyes.

"They especially hate books written in English." Soái Cũ's voice grew louder, and he pounded his fist on the table. "Students went door to door, making sure we had burned them all!"

I felt a pang of guilt that we had taken the place of

Soái Cũ and Kiểm and their family on the boat.

Ma must have felt the same way because she leaned forward and whispered, "Will you try to get on the next boat?"

Soái Kiểm turned to face Ma. "It's hard to know what is best, my sister. So many are desperate to leave. There's not enough food. Hunger has driven the poorest *người hoa* to sell their identification cards."

"Why doesn't everyone leave?"

"It's not that easy, Yen, to leave everything you have, even if most of what you had has been taken away. Most people do not have the courage to leave everything they have known for something even more uncertain. For some it's better to stay and deal with the evil that they know. And for some, their ties to our motherland are too deep."

My thoughts briefly wandered to Bác Minh. "What I can't understand is why, at the same time that we are being forced to leave because we are *người hoa*, they punish us for being traitors when we try to leave."

"Enough of this," said Soái Kiểm. "You're looking pale, Yen. Follow me to the exam room. I examined Quang already. It's your turn. I want to make sure you're good and strong for the journey."

Soái Kiểm's office was a single room located at the front of their house. It was common for doctors to practise from home. At the far end of the room was a narrow cot covered by a flat bamboo mat. A notepad and a few medical instruments lay atop a small wooden desk. Against a wall of peeling green paint was a small glass medicine cabinet that had pill bottles, but no Tiger balm. I was relieved. I couldn't possibly stand being pinched and coined the way Ma would do.

Soái Kiểm sat me down on the cot and felt my wrist. Then she listened intently to my chest and back with her stethoscope.

"You've got a good strong heart," she assured me. At that moment, Hieu and Anh came into the exam room to say goodbye before they went off to their afternoon classes. They were dressed in their school uniforms, topped with red caps.

"No point sitting around here, Yen," said Soái Kiểm. "Go learn something with them."

I eagerly grabbed my notebook, excited to have my chance to go to school again, even for just one day. But, my heart sank seeing so many people loitering about amidst the piles of garbage strewn along the streets. The stench stretched all the way up Tran Huong Dao Street.

"Many are now homeless," Hieu whispered. "When the soldiers take a fancy to your home, they march in and kick you out, just like that. No explanation."

I averted my eyes. Pedestrians, bicycles, minibuses and

xe lôi weaved in all directions, especially near Cho Ben Thanh market. But there was little spirit, as people carried on with their lives listlessly.

Green-uniformed officials with guns dangling from their backs marched past us at Independence Palace, and we picked up our pace.

"A tanker crashed through those gates—" Hieu pointed out.

"—on the day of the *giải phóng*, the liberation," finished Anh.

"Don't call it *giải phóng*!" Hieu snapped. "Don't listen to our teachers."

"My teachers are nice!" Anh said. "They teach us to understand the revolution—the history, and how to be a good person and help other people with love, to have dedication for our country."

"Anh, you don't know what you're saying."

"I do too. I like being part of the Red Capper group. I'm one of the best in my group."

"So those are Red Cappers' uniforms you're wearing?" I asked.

"They don't question us when we wear these uniforms. Everybody has to show their support for the revolution. Nobody dares challenge the northern army.

I felt a chill in the humid air. As we walked through downtown, we passed the Cathedral Notre-Dame de Saigon and Saigon Central Buu Dien. Covered in the colours of our new flag, they seemed to have lost their beauty and elegance.

We stopped at a house tucked away in a narrow alley. I was confused.

"This doesn't look like a school," I said.

"We aren't going to school today," Anh said. "This is where our lessons are."

"But aren't you dressed for school?"

"It's just a cover," whispered Hieu. "Our parents don't want us to get in trouble for coming here. This is where we take our Cantonese lessons. We can't talk about the lessons because the government forbids them."

Hieu opened the gates a crack, and I slipped in behind them. My knees were shaking.

SHORE

Maybe it was the desperate way Soái Kiểm held onto me that morning that made me feel agitated and queasy. Maybe it was how Ma and Soái Cũ clung to each other, or the tears in their eyes, which made me grieve along with them. Maybe it was the sticks of incense that were burning in the urn. Why did this freedom that they spoke of stir such a sense of loss? Would we never see them again?

Tòa Cũ's wife, Tòa Kiểm, and their sixteen-year-old son were there too.

"We are your family," I overheard Tòa Kiểm say to Tòa Cũ. "It is not your responsibility to take care of her children too."

But Tòa Cũ said, "I made a promise to our father on his deathbed that I would take care of my little sister."

Tòa Kiểm made a face and tossed some packaged food into our bags. She wasn't very pleasant to any of us.

When the time came, we followed Tòa Cũ to the bus terminal, keeping enough distance between his family and ours so as not to draw attention to ourselves. But with Quang and Tien's short little legs, we moved slowly and were at risk of being left behind.

"Hurry up!" Tòa Kiểm snapped at me, more than once.

Thankfully, Tòa Cũ was keeping an eye out for us. When they boarded the bus, I heard him say to the driver, "Please wait for the lady in the brown shirt with the three children."

We rode in silence through the crowded streets of Saigon. All I could do was stare out the window, watching the *xe lôi*, bicycles, and some motorbikes criss-cross from all around us. Dilapidated buildings lined the roads, strung together by low-lying electrical lines. Street vendors lined the sides of the road.

Tòa Cũ did not tell us our destination. If we happened to get caught, then there would be nothing to reveal. When Tien asked Ma where we were going, Ma only whispered, "To freedom." Soon Tien gave up asking, and the monotony of the ride lulled her to sleep.

After crossing by ferry across the Mekong, we somehow managed to elude the checkpoints and transfer to a smaller bus in Ben Tre. The driver seemed to know Tòa Cũ, and had been expecting us. The bus coursed over bumpy highways and rugged winding roads that made Quang green in the face.

Then it stopped. I sat up anxiously in my seat and looked out the window at the tall grass surrounding us.

We hurried off the bus and it drove away, leaving us at the side of a desolate road.

"Are we here, Tòa Cũ?" I asked. Light rain fell from the grey sky. "There's nothing here."

"Follow me," Tòa Cũ said. We walked through the bushes to the edge of the river. A small barge sat waiting for us. On it were six others. There was an elderly man, a middle-aged couple and three young men. They had two small suitcases between the six of them. We nodded to each other.

The barge sputtered slowly down the long winding river. By the time we got off, it was dark and the rain had tapered off.

Tòa Cũ guided us some distance by the light of the moon, through a forested area to an abandoned temple nestled in between palm leaves that rustled in the soft night breeze.

"This is it," he sad. "We're at the edge of a fishing village near the mouth of the sea. We will leave from here tomorrow night. One boat left earlier tonight, two more tomorrow."

In the shadows I could make out slumping, slouching, clumping shapes scattered all around the temple floor.

Tòa Cũ and his family headed to one end of the temple, and we found a corner in the foyer to rest in. Ma helped

Tien and Quang step over those who slept on the ground.

Ma placed her handbag beneath Quang's head while Tien's head rested on her lap. There was no room for me to stretch out, so I curled into a ball, using my arms as a pillow. It was impossible to sleep though, as more people arrived throughout the night. The wind howled.

Tòa Cũ was up early the next morning, busy taking headcounts and identifying those who would go with him. There so many people. People of all ages, from an infant child still nursing to the old man who had come on the barge with us.

"Have you ever been out to sea, Tòa Cũ?" I asked. He finally had a quiet moment to himself while Tòa Kiểm was napping.

"This will be my first time."

"Is it safe?"

He hesitated, but smiled. "We have an experienced captain."

"Do you know how long before we get to Ma-lay-sia?"

"If the weather holds, we should be in Malaysia in two days and two nights."

"Are Muoi and Lam there?"

"Yes, they should be there waiting for us."

I trusted him.

Tien and Quang played with two boys their own age.

"Are they your boys?" Ma asked the man leaning against the wall next to us, watching the children. He was quiet and poised. He explained how he had to leave his wife at home because she was pregnant and didn't want to be at sea. I could see hope glowing in his eyes as he spoke of ways she and their newborn could later join him and the boys.

Ma gazed into the distance as he spoke. She was thinking of Muoi and Lam. The thought of seeing Muoi and Lam again, of being able to go to school again, that gave me hope.

I began to feel restless inside the temple and decided to wander. The shore of the river was muddy. As I meandered, the sounds of waves swelled louder, the river became wider the farther I walked. The water was calm. The sound of the waves lapping the beach was soothing.

I ducked between tree branches and stopped in my tracks. A small brown suitcase lay on the ground ahead of me. It seemed odd that it would just be sitting there. It must have fallen off one of the boats and washed ashore.

The closer I got to the suitcase, beyond the last branches, the more I could see. I gasped. Not far from where I stood, a man was carrying the small body of a child, lifeless. Trinh's face flashed before me. I froze. Pieces of broken wood washed onto the shore. Nearby, other men hauled more bodies that the sea had returned to the land.

The man carried the child away in his arms, and behind him I noticed a woman on the ground with skin as white as porcelain, hair with silver locks as shiny as jewels. It was a face familiar, yet strange. My heart tore in two.

It was Cô Sáu. Cô Sáu still dressed in her dusky blue outfit, blood marking the corners of her eyes and pale lips. I could not breathe. The ocean waves roared in my head. I wanted to cry, but I couldn't. I wanted to scream, but I couldn't.

Suddenly, someone grabbed me from behind. "You shouldn't be here. Go back," the man said. "Go away!"

I started running. As fast as I could, I ran.

"Go away," the voice screamed at me. "Go away!"

I could not scream.

BOARDING

Nam Mô A Di Dà Phật, Nam Mô A Di Dà Phật. The phrase once again echoed in my head. Why was I praying so much when I no longer had faith in Buddha? I trembled inside. My heart would not stop pounding against my chest. I found Ma and broke down.

"I don't want to go," I sobbed. "We can't go."

"What happened?" Ma gripped my shoulders with both hands. But I couldn't tell her what I had seen. I could not find the words. For the first time in a long time, she drew me close to her, stroked my hair, held me and whispered, "We will be okay."

I wasn't sure if she said that to comfort me or as a prayer. Eventually I curled into a ball in the corner. I could not eat or speak for the rest of the day. I could not bring myself to tell Ma what I had seen, but she might have known. If any others knew, nothing was said, but I saw Tòa Cũ speaking to one of the local fishermen. Tòa Cũ made no mention of the fate of the boat that had left the night before, but surely word had travelled quickly. I watched Tòa Cũ like a hawk all day. His shoulders were drooped, his face a mix of fear and melancholy.

By late afternoon, the boats had rolled in. Uncle said our boat was the second one. The winds were picking up as they had the night before and, to our dismay, dark clouds were rolling in too. I wasn't the only one watching the sky. I could hear murmured prayers begging the heavens for mercy.

As night fell, another hundred people emerged from the woods. Was it possible to fit all these people into just two small wooden fishing vessels?

Ma finally said, "It is time to go."

Everyone shuffled down to the muddy shore. The two fishing boats waited stoically in the dark, with wooden planks stretched from deck to shore.

Four green-uniformed officials stood between us and the boats. *They are sending you to your death*, howled the wind.

I yanked Ma's hand to pull her back. The wind howled louder. *Turn around*, it said.

The officials held flashlights to a list of names. Hanging from their belts were large menacing guns.

"I expect you have all paid your dues," said one of them.

The officials called people up one by one, waving the flashlights between their faces and their identity cards. I wanted to scream that we were all walking to our deaths, but I could not.

The man who was leaving his pregnant wife behind bid us farewell and he and his two sons climbed onto the first boat. They were among the last to get on, and the boat swayed back and forth from the weight of the people overflowing on the top deck.

As the first boat sputtered away, the officials began roll call for the second boat. A woman pushed through the crowd when she and her child were called. I recognized that woman—it was the haughty woman from the Ca Mau market. From *his* house. She had tied her son's wrist to her own. In her other hand was a large suitcase.

Why was she leaving alone? Where was *he*? She wasn't *người hoa*. She must have fake documents. How many of these people had fake documents too? I watched as she stepped onto the boat. I hated the idea of breathing the same air as her.

Boarding was slow. The wind grew stronger. Palm trees swayed. The dark sky rumbled.

My knees wobbled when, at long last, our names were called. As we stood up, a commotion broke out in front of us. There was loud hollering and splashing. Flashlights shone frantically in all directions. The soldiers dragged two men back to shore. They threw the men to the ground and started beating on them, punching and kicking. Ma covered Quang's and Tien's eyes. I turned away.

"Stowaways," shouted an official. "No payment, no passage."

I caught some movement at the corner of my eyes. Another man circled the crowd, trying to sneak on board. He wore a jade pendant around his neck.

"I don't want to go, Ma," I wailed. "We're going to die. I don't want to go." Tien started to cry too, even louder.

"If you can't control them, you will not board!" shouted an officer. Ma apologized to the officers, and when the stowaway with the pendant had boarded from the side, I turned off the tears.

I thought we would be seated on the top deck with Tòa Cũ, but we were instead directed down into the pit, into the hold where the fish were normally stowed.

Then they pulled the planks, closed the lid and left us in the dark. It took a minute for my eyes to adjust. A couple of small light bulbs were strung precariously from the ceiling of the hold, emitting a dim light. A long plastic tube hung down from above to funnel a little fresh air to the hundred or so refugees trapped below.

Then the engines sputtered and rumbled. I held my breath as we jerked to a start. Rain pounded ever louder. The water grew choppier the further we sailed, tossing us against the hull and each other. We were at the mercy of the sea.

We had not sailed far before cries and panic broke out from the top deck. "The first boat is down! The first boat is gone!"

"Turn around!" begged voices in the darkness. "The waves are too strong. We will sink!"

I clung to Ma and the children. My heart shattered at the thought of the man whose wife would always be waiting for his call to join him. A call that would never come.

This must be how it feels right before you die, I thought, *when you have accepted your fate.*

SEA

Deep within the belly of the boat, everyone cried. I wanted to cry too, but couldn't. I had no more tears. I could easily have been that child on the beach, or one of the people in the first boat. I was afraid we would never see Muoi and Lam again.

After some time the crying trailed off, and for a time there was no sound other than the struggling engine fighting against the waves that tossed us against each other. Then prayers began. "*Nam Mô A Di Dà Phật, Nam Mô A Di Dà Phật.*" But I refused to pray. If our prayers had been helping, the sea wouldn't be ripping our boat apart.

Tien was curled in Ma's lap, her eyes half-opened. Tien was tougher than I thought. Through it all, she made no complaints and showed no fear. Back and forth we swayed, up and down we rose and fell. One wave after another would hit and toss us around. Now it was not just the boat that was bruised and battered.

The sound of retching and the smell of vomit made me gag. The air had turned sour. Quang dry-heaved a few times then threw up all over his legs. There was no remedy or relief. We had nowhere to move. There was no room to straighten our legs or stand upright. We were like fish, packed tightly into the bowels of the ship.

Across from me, separated by one dim swinging bulb, sat a couple with four daughters around my age and older. The sisters clung to each other. All had long lashes and thick long hair that draped their shoulders and backs. Beyond them, tucked in a corner, was the stowaway with the jade pendant. He had his eyes closed in meditation.

Tien continued to sleep, unfazed. Quang threw up again and then just dry-heaved over and over until he cried out in pain. Tòa Cũ and his family had no idea how awful the putrid air was down in the hold. Ma raised her voice to the ceiling. "Please let my son up on deck, to get some fresh air."

No response from above.

She shouted louder. "He is very sick. Please, have some compassion."

There was still no answer.

"Shout even louder," said a man next to us. "It would be heartless of them to not let the poor child up." It was the man who had been on the barge with us. His elderly father was leaning against his grandsons.

"Is your father doing alright?" Ma asked. "Does he need to go up too?"

"He is okay. He is old, but he is tough," the man said. "We could not leave him behind." His wife, on the other hand, looked worried. The sea was more unforgiving than any of us could have imagined.

Ma raised her voice again. "Have some compassion for my boy."

Either they could not hear us or they heard and chose not to listen. Frustrated, I got up and worked my way to the ladder through the maze of people. I lifted the lid and stuck my head above deck to get my uncle's attention.

"Quang is really sick, Tòa Cū. Can we please bring him on deck?"

"There's no room for anyone else on deck," Tòa Kiểm said.

But Tòa Cū nodded. "Just a few minutes."

The rocking of the boat made it difficult to manoeuvre through the tangle of legs, baggage and pools of vomit. We tripped and nearly fell, but someone caught us and steadied us. It was the stowaway with the jade pendant. Other hands propelled us forward and upward.

The rise and fall of the boat were more dramatic on top, but the fresh air was a welcome relief. Quang's colour returned as he inhaled the fresh sea breeze. My stomach settled too. It looked like the storm was passing.

Through the cluster of people on deck, I saw the profile of the haughty woman and her son sitting mere metres away. She must have paid extra for a spot on deck. My bitterness and curiosity grew. Where was *he*? Perhaps she had abandoned *him*. Maybe *he* was dead? Despite the darkness of the night, I could see the similarities between this little boy and his father. For a moment I wished they had been on the first boat, but a flash of guilt came over me when my eyes fell on the young boy. His name was Hoang, I remembered. If only *he* had been a better person, so much would have been different.

Quang coughed and stirred a little in my arms. Then I realized that Quang would still be orphaned on the streets if we had stayed with *him*. Quang was trouble he wouldn't take. I leaned back and held Quang a little tighter. He was not that much trouble. There was a reason things happened the way they did. Some people appeared in our lives at the right time, the right place, just when we needed them— like the coconut lady.

I looked up into the sky. The clouds had dispersed and an ebony bowl covered us with a million stars that glittered in the night. I felt small, insignificant. Our little boat was a mere pinpoint under the great expanse with no beginning and no end between sea and sky.

In that moment, I felt a powerful presence, too elusive to comprehend and too pervasive to ignore.

DRiFTiNG

What should have taken two days had turned to three, then four. The storm had blown us off course. On the fourth day at sea, the motor sputtered, choked, then went silent.

"What happens now?" I asked Ma as she wiped the sweat off Tien's forehead.

"They'll figure out something," Ma said. I wasn't convinced.

"We should've arrived by now," said the mother of the four girls. Her voice was shaky and weak. "How will anyone find our tiny boat in this big sea?"

"We're doomed, we're doomed," cried another woman, but others hushed her.

"Are we going to die?" Quang whispered to Ma. Tien frowned at him. I was upset by the question too, but I waited for Ma's answer.

"God is watching over us," Ma said.

Nam Mô A Di Dà Phật, I prayed.

"We should toss you overboard." A man was yelling at the stowaway. "We don't have enough food and water for you."

"Leave him alone!" I said, upset that someone would threaten the man who had helped us.

"There's no point fighting each other," said another man. "We all have one fate."

Without the movement of the boat, the air had grown even more stale. The lights no longer worked, but the lid of the hold had been lifted to let some air and light in. My muscles were cramped but I could not complain. Our boat rose and fell with the waves in no particular direction. Those who could swim were allowed to jump briefly into the sea to wash up. We craved rain to replenish our drinking water.

"Would you be so kind as to give us a little more food and water?" someone asked, trying to get the attention of those on deck.

"You've had your share," called a voice from above. "We don't know how many days we'll be at sea. We can't waste any food."

"But I need more water to nurse," a young mother pleaded.

"Have some compassion," begged a fourth.

The stowaway made no demands. I could see that he

drank sparingly and ate little, picking at the grains of rice from discarded wrappers thrown his way.

"Have a bite." Ma offered the rations to us, but I shook my head and passed it on to Quang and Tien. Hunger was an old acquaintance that no longer frightened me. The children also shook their heads. Ma stuck the small amount of rice back into her bag and pulled out a container of water. It was nearly empty. "Drink. You need to drink even if you cannot eat."

I looked over to the old man beside us. His daughter-in-law was asking the people around them to spare some room. "He needs to lie down. Please understand." His breathing was heavy. He moaned and muttered words that made no sense.

"Is he ill?" I asked.

"He's not feeling very well." The woman tried giving him water, but he was too weak to swallow. "I don't know what we'll do if we don't make it to land soon."

I sat holding my knees against my chest and kept watch on the old man, wishing that I could do something to help. *Perhaps I can will him back to health*, I thought. His breathing got heavier though, and by the next day he barely responded to his name.

Like fuel thrust at a dwindling flame, a commotion flared up above us.

"There's a fishing boat!" someone shouted.

I could feel our boat lean as the people on deck shifted in excitement to one side. They hollered, "Please save us!"

"They're coming to help us!"

People cheered. In the hold, we rejoiced too. Our boat came to a sudden stop when the other vessel bumped into ours.

But then shouting erupted. The voices of strange men barked orders in a language we could not understand.

"What's happening?" I trembled.

"We just need help," I heard Tòa Cũ's calm voice say. There was a thud and a thump. Someone had fallen onto the floor of the deck. Cries pierced the air. We were being attacked. There was more shouting and screaming.

"Pirates," someone murmured.

I tried not to breathe, but my heart was thumping so loud, I was sure it could be heard on deck. Quang covered his ears and Tien tightened her clutch on Ma. Ma squeezed our hands, warning us to sit still, to keep quiet, hoping that whatever was happening above would stop there.

The deck creaked.

The young girls and women screamed, cried and pleaded. "Ma! Ba!"

"Spare our daughters! Please! Mercy please!"

My heart pounded faster. The pirates' laughter sent a chill down my spine.

Three men slid down through the hole into our pit. These pirates were scraggly ordinary-looking men, but the viciousness in their eyes brought terror to our hearts. One wielded a knife and a gun; the other, a hammer and a large brown sack. They growled to each other and laughed. The first waved his gun and knife around at each of us. The man with the sack crouched down and made his way through the crowd, stomping on men and women alike, tearing off earrings, necklaces and watches, and grabbing whatever else he could find. I slid Ma's handbag underneath my legs. I had to protect my notebook.

"No! I have nothing," said one of our men as the pirate yanked at a bag hidden underneath him. He swung the hammer at the man's head. There was a loud crack and blood gushed out from the man's forehead. The pirate pulled out several gold taels from the bag and struck the man again.

I tried to signal to the stowaway that his pendant was showing, but the pirate came over to us.

"We have nothing," Ma cried. I closed my eyes, paralyzed with fear, and prepared to be beaten.

"Leave the women and children alone," the stowaway said. I dared not look in his direction. The pirate turned to search for the person who had spoken up. He pummelled the nearest man with his hammer, then shouted at us.

I don't know what he said, but his partner laughed. I shuddered.

The pirate eyed me up and down, but I didn't move. Suddenly, he reached down and seized one of the four sisters. Her father and mother cried out and clung to their daughter, but the pirate stomped and kicked them, pounding their hands with the hammer until they lost their grip.

The other pirates dragged more girls out of the hold. I could not breathe. I was within reach and it could have been me they grabbed. The mothers and fathers bellowed in pain, hearing the screams of their daughters from the pirates' boat.

Finally, they returned the girls to us. Their shirts and slacks were torn, lips swollen, bodies trembling. The mother of the four sisters released an agonizing wail that cleaved our hearts in two. Her sisters sobbed as their mother clutched her daughter close.

I wept quietly. I could not fathom their pain, her pain.

When I opened my eyes the next morning, the elderly man had stopped breathing. His family's mourning numbed me.

They wrapped him in cloth and carried him out of the hold. Then I heard the heavy splash of his body being dropped into the sea.

I could not cry. My tears were spent. Gone with him into the sea was my hope.

ECHOES

With hope gone, we had nothing left. We were all waiting to die. Another day passed. And another.

There was despair on the sunken faces of many, but others were too weak and battered to care. Their faces were empty. If we were to be found then surely someone would have found us by now.

Tòa Cũ came down to check on us once. His forehead was bruised. I could tell he was consumed with the guilt of having the blood of all these lives on his hands.

"I promised Ba Ba I would protect you, Siu Heung," he said, his voice fragile, desolate, grief-stricken. "But I have brought you and the children to this end. I should never have led you into this."

Ma shook her head. Tòa Cũ had done his best to help us when he could, to get us through the hard years. "We had to try for the sake of the children," Ma said. "That's the best we could do for them. Ba Ba would be proud, my brother. The rest is up to God and Buddha."

Tòa Cũ gently stroked my cheek and the children's hair, and disappeared. Was hope gone for him too?

The children were too famished and weak to cry. All was quiet. The smell of death lingered in the air, slowly extinguishing any embers of hope that still glowed inside us. But a feeling of levity and peace washed over me as we snuggled in Ma's embrace. The soft rhythm of her heart lulled me into a daze.

I had no strength to move. I didn't want to break away from the comfort of Ma's arms, but then she unwrapped us from her arms and shook us awake. I had no choice but to straighten up.

"Something's happening," Ma said. She rose to her knees. "I think someone's found us." Ma clasped her hands together in gratitude to the heavens.

Nam Mô A Di Dà Phật, Nam Mô A Di Dà Phật.

"Our prayers have been answered," someone whispered.

I craned my neck and listened intently to the sounds from above. The people around us stirred with excitement and relief. Footsteps drummed over our heads.

"Look at their flag. It's a Malaysian ship."

Someone shouted, "Land must be near!"

"We have made it, we survived!"

Men and women alike started to weep tears of joy. Even the family with four daughters smiled. The stowaway opened his eyes. They were like Cô Thanh's eyes.

There was distant shouting. Ma recognized the words, they were in Mandarin. Others on our boat understood Mandarin too, and relayed the message. "They're throwing us a line. Grab the rope!"

I could hear Tòa Cū's voice giving orders to work quickly to tie the rope to the bow of our boat. "They'll pull us to shore."

I smiled at Ma. I imagined how beautiful Malaysia would be. How wonderful it would be to set foot on new land.

"We can eat a big bowl of rice tonight," said Tien.

"Yes, I'm sure we will," Ma said as our boat started moving again.

"Maybe I can have a toy of my own," added Quang. He was paler than all of us, having lost so much fluid. There was so much we could do once we reached land.

"And we'll see Muoi and Lam again," I said.

Ma smiled at last. "Yes, we will."

After the wave of excitement settled, the mood in the hold suddenly changed.

"Why are they pulling us so fast?"

"Something is not right."

"What's happening?" I asked. My heart racing again.

Ma shook her head and held on to us tightly again. "I don't know. Tòa Cū will take care of it."

Someone shouted down to us, "They're pulling us

farther out to sea!" A couple of men crawled up to the deck to see for themselves.

"Why would they do that?" I asked. I was breathing so hard I was almost out of breath.

Ma said, "They do not want us in their country."

Over the hysterical voices, I could hear Tòa Cũ yell, "Cut the rope! Cut the rope!" There was clamouring and shouting above.

Out of nowhere, a gunshot exploded outside—a warning shot. We stiffened, but the people above didn't stop what they were doing. Another shot. Then another.

Faster and faster, our boat was being dragged back out to sea. I was in shock. We had travelled all this way to find refuge.

"Water's coming in!" someone shouted. A shot had made a hole in the side of the boat. "Water's coming in!"

"Get on deck!"

We scrambled onto our feet in the tangle of arms and limbs to make our way out of the hold. Ma tried to hang on to our hands, but the crush of people dragged us apart. In the chaos, I caught a glimpse of the stowaway helping Tien and Quang up, but I was being pushed farther and farther back.

"Ma!" I screamed, but my screams were drowned out.

I thought I could hear Ma calling for me, but I could not see her. I could not catch my breath. Then the screams of panic got louder. The boat was leaning. I grabbed a post by the ladder to keep from falling over. The bottleneck out of the pit was choking us.

"Oh my God, we're all going to die!"

The boat was tipping on to its side and the farther it tilted, the more I could hear the splash of bodies dropping like pebbles into the sea. I clung desperately to the post.

Then we were engulfed. Everything went silent except for the rush of water pouring in. I could see the horror in the eyes of everyone still trapped below.

The next thing I knew I was tumbling out of the hold. Frantically I propelled my arms as fast and as hard as I could, the way Lam had taught me, before the boat could belly-up completely on top of me.

I erupted from the water, gasping hungrily for air. I caught sight of a large empty water canister, floating within reach, and wrapped my arms around it. My eyes darted around, looking for Ma. That's when I spotted the woman with her son tied to her wrist. She was struggling to keep her head above water. Her son had lost consciousness. I wanted to turn away, but Trinh's face flashed before me. I had to help.

"Hold on to this canister," I shouted at the woman. Instead she grabbed my arm, pushing me down to keep afloat.

"I can't—" I gasped, spitting out water.

She would not let go. The unconscious child weighed us both down.

My heart thundered against my chest. I gasped desperately for air. I could not scream. The more I tried, the heavier my chest became. I sank deeper and deeper with the woman and her child.

Hatred in the heart is as heavy as stones in your soul, Bác Minh's voice echoed in my head. *The weight will sink you.*

All at once I found the strength to slip out of her grip. I wrapped my arms around her chest and kicked the water vigorously to propel us to the surface. Then a set of hands reached in and grabbed the woman and child. The jade pendant floated on the surface as he took the woman and child from my hands.

The upturned boat was still afloat. The stowaway laid the little boy on the hull that was barely above water, and pressed on the boy's chest until he spat out water. It was a relief to see the rise and fall of Hoang's chest. Holding on to the boat beside him was his mother.

I exhaled and looked around. The sea was peppered with people struggling to keep afloat, some clinging to large plastic jugs, others to luggage or any other object.

"Ma?" I called out.

The stowaway pointed. To my relief I saw Tien and Quang hanging on to the hull on the other side of the boat.

Ma was with them. Where was Tòa Cũ? At any moment the sea would swallow the boat, taking us all down.

The late afternoon sun beat down on us. In the distance, the Malaysian ship had turned around and was coming toward us, fast.

Its sailors were standing on the bow of the ship. They looked just like the Vietnamese soldiers we were running from.

"What are they doing?" someone shouted.

"They're coming back to finish us off."

The people in the water splashed frantically, trying to clear from the ship's path.

But the ship slowed and came to a stop.

The officers threw lifesavers down into the water, then unrolled a rope ladder down its side. They reached down and plucked the stranded people from the sea, one by one. But it was already too late for far too many. Of the hundreds that had come on Tòa Cũ's boat searching for a better future, only a few dozen had survived. None of us had known that the cost of freedom would be so high.

Everything went blurry. Water welled in my eyes, then it streamed down my cheeks without end.

I don't know how long it took, but by the time they pulled the last survivor from the water, the sun had become an amber fireball hanging over the horizon.

The lighting softened the faces of our rescuers, and I no longer shuddered when they stood over us. Someone who spoke Mandarin told us it was the Malaysian Coast Guard. They had been given orders to rescue us after their failed attempt to pull us out to international waters.

As the ship picked up speed, we huddled tightly together on the deck to keep warm in the cool breeze. Tien and Quang sat quietly in Ma's arms. I rested my head on her shoulder, knowing that Cô Thanh would be happy her son made it to safety, and that the woman and Hoang were somewhere among the survivors. Tòa Cũ was not on the ship, but I sensed he was near, watching over us as he had always done and as he had promised Ông Ngoại.

Rain started to fall softly. I tilted my head back and felt the gentle drops on my face, tasting the sweetness of the water. I closed my eyes and the wind whispered, "You are free."

I stood up. The setting sun bathed our new land in an orange glow, and a deep feeling of peace settled over me.

AUTHOR'S NOTE

After the fall of Saigon, thousands of Vietnamese were executed and over one million were sent to prison or re-education camps, where thousands more died. The ensuing conflicts with Cambodia and China only made living conditions worse for the people. Repression was especially severe for the ethnic Chinese (*người hoa*) as they were stripped of their land, their properties confiscated, resulting in economic hardship.

Between 1978 and 1979, there was a mass exodus of refugees from Vietnam, Cambodia and Laos by land and sea, with over a million Vietnamese fleeing the war-ravaged country on small rickety fishing boats, crammed with hundreds of refugees. These were the "boat people." Thousands did not survive the storms, and the hundreds of thousands more who did, suffered starvation, illness and attacks from pirates. Malaysia, Thailand, Hong Kong, the Philippines, Indonesia and Singapore were the first countries of refuge.

Even though *A Grain of Rice* is a work of fiction, many of the events I describe are loosely based on my family's escape from Vietnam. I was born in a caul and the youngest of six, much like Tien. Perhaps I also had the protection of *Mụ bà*, as the boat that left just before ours crashed at sea too, taking the lives of all on board, but ours did not. If it were not for the courage of our mother, our lives would have turned out much differently. She sacrificed everything for her children.

We landed on the shores of Malaysia, and were held in a refugee camp, where we received daily rations of food from the Red Cross. We had to climb a nearby mountain to chop wood for building a shelter, and Ma prayed every day that we would find a new home. After eight long months, we received word that Canada would take us. Our Canadian sponsors had specifically asked to support a family like ours—with a widowed mother and six children, the kind of family that no one else wanted.

I am a doctor and a writer, and I have three young children of my own. In 2016, we helped sponsor two families fleeing the conflict in Syria. According to the Office of the United Nations High Commissioner for Refugees (UNHCR), there remain 65 million people forcibly displaced from their homes due to war and conflict. Half of these are children.

GLOSSARY

Áo bà ba:	Traditional Vietnamese two-piece ensemble
Bà ngoại:	Maternal grandmother
Bác:	A term to address someone older than their parents
Bánh bao:	Meat or sweet-filled steamed buns
Bánh bèo:	Steamed little rice cakes garnished usually with shrimp, scallions and eaten with fish sauce
Bánh xèo:	Vietnamese fried crêpes
Cô:	A term to address an adult woman younger than their parents
Cậu:	A term to address an adult man younger than their parents
Cóc chua:	Ambarella (sour)
Dòng:	Vietnamese dollar
Giải phóng:	"Liberation" of southern Vietnam
Mụ bà:	Guardian Deity of Children
Nam Mô A Di Dà Phật:	A prayer chant expressing one's faith in Buddha
Người hoa:	Vietnamese citizens of Chinese descent
Ông ngoại:	Maternal grandfather
Phở:	A popular Vietnamese rice noodle soup, made usually with beef or chicken meat and broth
Tầng địa ngục:	Levels of hell, usually believed to be 18
Xe lôi:	Rickshaws
Xoài chua:	Mango (sour)